ALSO BY LINDA RAWLINS

The Misty Point Mystery Series

Misty Manor

Misty Point

Misty Winter

Misty Treasure

Misty Revenge

The Rocky Meadow Mystery Series

The Bench

Fatal Breach

Sacred Gold

The Elizabeth Brooks Mystery Series

Midnight Shift

MISTY RETREAT

A MISTY POINT MYSTERY
BOOK 6

LINDA RAWLINS

RIVERBENCH PUBLISHING, LLC

MISTY RETREAT

Misty Retreat
A Misty Point Mystery

By Linda Rawlins

E-Book: 978-0-9600549-4-7
Paperback: 978-0-9600549-5-4

Discover other titles by Linda Rawlins at
www.lindarawlins.com

For

Linda H, Sue H, Mary S, Louann N, Cathy S
for their dedication to
medicine, love, and friendship.

AUTHOR'S NOTE

I would like to thank Lt. M. Sharp, of the New Jersey State Park Police for patient advice and assistance with writing this novel. According to their website, The New Jersey State Park Police patrol and protect the State's 54 Parks, Forests, and Recreational Areas and 130 Natural Trust Preserves which encompass approximately 450,000 acres and are visited by more than 18 million people each year. The New Jersey State Park Police are empowered with the same law enforcement authority as all New Jersey municipal, county, and state police officers, dealing with the same issues that other law enforcement agencies deal with daily. The New Jersey State Park Police also have an excellent record at search and rescue on all terrains with search and cadaver dogs as well as other means, including helicopters. They have their own detective unit and handle their own investigations but also provide mutual aid between local, state, county, and private teams when necessary.

Please note that all errors, exaggerations, creative license, and difference of fact, if any, are entirely the fault of the author.

ACKNOWLEDGMENTS

It is one thing to write a book, it is quite another to publish a novel. Misty Retreat is my tenth novel and, once again, I would like to thank all who have supported, led, and pushed me on my writing journey. For without them, I never would have reached this important milestone. I was recently reminded of my excitement upon hearing for the first time, that someone beyond a family member, purchased one of my books. The sheer honor that someone would want to read my words. That thrill has never diminished! I offer gracious thanks to my many readers, librarians, booksellers, and friends, far and wide, that I have met through writing.

I would be remiss if I didn't thank my crew, tribe, and street team. To my first readers - Joyce, Sandy, Anita, Lorraine, Joe, and Krista. Your feedback and attention to detail is amazing and I am forever grateful.

To my mom, Joyce - your editing experience is still superior to most.

To the crew at Riverbench Publishing - Matt, Ashley, and Krista. You do an amazing job on everything that holds the entire writing process together.

To Dr. Joe for keeping everything spinning and making my coffee daily to keep me going!

To my special readers who always support and push me harder! I promise I will continue to strive!

The first ten were just the beginning.

1

"What a beautiful day."

Nick stayed silent as he shifted his beach chair in the sand.

"What's wrong, Nick?" Megan closed her eyes and took a deep breath of salty ocean air, as if she knew what was coming.

"I can't take it anymore. I'm getting restless," Nick said quietly from her side.

"I've noticed, but I'm sorry, Nick. You don't really have a choice. You're off duty until you heal." Megan Stanford watched his face for signs of distress and then tilted hers toward the sun.

Nick flicked his eyes in her direction before he pulled his sunglasses down. "Don't get me wrong. I'm grateful I'm alive and even more grateful I was able to move to Misty Manor from the hospital."

Megan turned and searched his face once again. "It's not everyday someone is poisoned like you were and lives to talk about it."

Nick nodded silently and then stared out toward the ocean.

Megan sighed as she turned to watch the ocean pound the shore. "It was easier for us to take care of you at Misty Manor."

"I know and I am appreciative. I just can't stand all this rest and relaxation." Nick leaned over, grabbed Megan's hand, and circled her fingers with his thumb. "Let's just enjoy this day."

Megan turned her chair so she could look directly at Nick Taylor, her boyfriend. He had lost weight since he was poisoned. The constant medical tests as well as the necessary antidote contributed to his loss of appetite. Some of his hair had initially fallen out and he had developed numbness in his feet. "It's been a scary six weeks and I'm happy you're feeling better."

"Me too," Nick said with a smile.

"I've noticed your appetite is returning and your hair has started to grow back. You must be feeling better if you're getting restless."

"That's true," Nick said with a small laugh.

"We're lucky to have a beach day like this in October." The day was perfect. One of those rare fall beach days that boasts perfect air and water temperatures with minimal crowds. Megan leaned over, picked up her water bottle and took a small sip. When she put the bottle back in the sand, she suppressed a small shudder and turned toward her boyfriend.

"It's hard to believe you almost died six weeks ago. You've done so well with the treatments, and you only have a couple of weeks left. You can do it." Megan smiled. "Besides, I think you enjoy being spoiled."

Nick laughed as he ran his fingers through the fine white sand. "Between your tender, loving care and Marie's cooking, it's been nothing but a dream."

"Yet, you hate it," Megan said with a wry smile as she cocked her head to the side.

Nick paused as his face fell. "No, I don't hate it. Not at all, but I don't feel like I have a purpose. I need to do something."

Megan quietly adjusted her hat to avoid sunburn on her face. She stared at the water, unable to form the words she had been thinking for the last six weeks. She was a rich woman and could easily afford to offer Nick a job, but he would never be kept. Neither one of them would ever have to work again except to run the foundation. Nick didn't have to rejoin the police department where his life was at risk daily, but he would never accept anything he didn't earn. If he couldn't work his way, he wasn't interested. They had already had this argument and Megan knew it hampered their relationship.

Megan Stanford was the granddaughter of Rose Stanford and the great-granddaughter of John Stanford, a sea captain who was given a large parcel of land on the coast of New Jersey, as a gift for completing an important transatlantic voyage, for a rich Philadelphia man, in the late 1800's. John built a lighthouse on the point, as well as a beautiful Grand Victorian Mansion, as a gift for his new wife, Mary. John named the Grand Victorian, Misty Manor, and the rest of the town, Misty Point. Over the last hundred years, the town had grown and prospered. Portions of the town were sold to accommodate year-round residents, as well as a boardwalk, and beach front buildings, but most of the town was still owned by the Stanford family. All was inherited by Megan when her grandmother, Rose, recently died. Megan had accepted her grandmother's request to remain the chair of the Stanford Foundation, which supported many of the charities in town, as well as the surrounding county.

"Nick, you could help run the foundation, but I would hate to have you start a position and then pull out a short time later and go back to work on the police force."

"I get it," Nick said with a nod in her direction. "We both know that is exactly what would happen."

"When is your next appointment with the doctor?"

"Monday," Nick said with a smile. "Hopefully, I won't need another test for a month or more. The last test showed no poison in my system, and the doctor wants to make sure he confirms everything before he lets me start working again."

A shadow crossed Megan's face as she quietly said, "I was so frightened when you were hospitalized. Thankfully, they were able to reverse the effects right away. How are your symptoms?"

Nick shrugged as he turned back to the ocean. "I still have some tingling or light numbness in my right leg."

"Yeah, but your hair and eyelashes are growing back. Your skin color is normal."

"And it's only been six weeks," Nick said, his voice thick with frustration.

Megan laughed. "To be honest, I thought you looked cute when you were blue."

Nick turned toward her with a frown. "Of all the antidotes in the world, I had to use one that turns your skin blue."

"I'm sorry, I didn't mean to make fun of you," Megan said as she squeezed his hand. "I'm purposely making light of things because watching you almost die was one of the scariest things that has ever happened to me. I don't want to be in that situation again and I don't know what I would have done if I had lost you."

"No one is losing anyone," Nick said as he swallowed. "I've just got to get back on my feet and up to speed. I need to start working out."

"You need to eat and gain some weight," Megan said with a shake of her head. "You're very close to your goal. Have you made a game plan for when you're released?"

"Not yet, but I have a meeting set up with Captain Davis. He called me earlier and wants to talk. I guess he received some paperwork from the doctor."

Megan smiled although her stomach knotted in silence. She didn't want him to return to work although she knew he'd be right back to the Misty Point Police Department the second he was cleared.

"When is your meeting?"

"Day after tomorrow," Nick said as he jumped up from his chair. "But in the meantime," he grabbed Megan's hand and dragged her down to the water's edge.

"Oh no, you don't." Megan momentarily escaped his grasp. Laughing as she ran, she let him catch up to her. He lifted her in his arms and made his way far enough into the ocean to plunge them both underneath the next wave. When it passed, they bobbed up in the water, but Nick continued to hold her close as they kissed and floated through the incoming waves.

2

M anhattan, NY - Antacus Pharmaceuticals

"SENSITIVITY TRAINING? What the hell are you talking about?"

"That's right, Bob. Sensitivity training. You're lucky we're not sending you to an official HR review. We'll try this first, but if it doesn't work, you'll be in their office next."

Bob took a deep breath as he looked past his boss and out the tall windows of the skyscraper. Beyond those windows were some of the most beautiful views of Manhattan. "I came here for my annual corporate review. You know, we joke around about goals for the next year, have a glass or two of bourbon and then go out for dinner. What the hell is going on?"

Dominic King sighed and leaned back in his plush leather chair. He looked down and straightened his tie before he spoke.

Bob waited patiently in the visitor chair on the other side of the desk. He had dressed in a Ralph Lauren suit as he was certain he and his boss would be on their way to a fancy Manhattan restaurant by now. His cuffs sported new diamond cufflinks. His legs were crossed, one foot resting on his opposite knee, brand new Italian leather shoes on his feet.

Dominic shrugged. "The corporate world has changed, you know that. We must poll the workers and check for problems. I don't think I was surprised that your name came up multiple times."

Bob Flowers burst out laughing. "You don't take that crap seriously, do you?"

"It doesn't matter what I think. Leadership is watching and your name was linked with certain disturbing traits, such as insensitivity, apathy, lack of compassion and being out of touch among others. There are allegations of drinking on the job. You're lucky no one called you sexist or racist or you would have already been out of here."

"You are serious," Bob repeated incredulously.

Dominic nodded. "Indeed I am. Your team thinks you're out of touch. You're in a high position in a pharmaceutical company and can't see the results of your work or the effect of your attitude on your colleagues or the patients and families we serve."

Bob blinked as he watched his boss. He uncrossed his legs and sat forward, his elbows on his knees and his face in his hands. "Okay, so what are you saying? Lay it out for me."

"After much discussion with the governing body, we are sending the managers with this type of review to a special retreat in New Jersey."

Bob frowned and sat straight up. "What kind of retreat and who the hell else is involved?"

Dominic smiled. "Like I said, it's a sensitivity retreat. You'll be there for a week. Each day you'll have certain tasks to accomplish."

"And then what? We get locked up in our hotel room after our HR talk and special buffet lunch in the ballroom?"

Dominic chuckled as he shook his head. "Oh Bob, that's exactly why you were the first one on the list. I guarantee you won't be going to a hotel."

Bob realized the meeting was over when his boss placed his file on the desk and stood up.

"You'll receive further instructions and the exact date of your retreat in a day or so. I want it understood that this retreat is mandatory to your continued employment in this company. We will meet again when you return and plan the next steps for your career."

Bob sat in his chair and stared for a moment, waiting for his boss to reveal their conversation was a prank. But that never happened.

Dominic walked around the desk and ushered Bob to the office door where his assistant was waiting. "Miss Horner, please escort Mr. Flowers to the elevator." He turned to Bob and said, "Watch your email. You'll receive explicit directions in a day or two. If you have questions, please reach out to Miss Horner and she'll provide any further information you may need."

Without realizing he was moving, Bob Flowers found himself in the hall staring at the closed door of Dominic King's office.

3

"Food's ready," Nick said as he handed a platter laden with hot dogs and hamburgers to Megan. She carefully walked up the stairs to the wraparound porch of Misty Manor and placed it on the table.

Marie hovered in the area, making sure the guests were happy with simple appetizers as well as beer or chilled wine. "None for you," Marie said and shooed both Dudley and Bella away from the table.

"Aww, the poor dogs," Megan said with a smile.

Marie turned to her and grinned. "Trust me, these dogs eat better than any of us."

Hands on the post, Tommy leaned over the porch railing and yelled. "Nick, turn off the grill and come up here. We're pouring the wine."

After closing the grill, Nick checked the propane tank and joined the group on the porch. When he reached the table, Tommy picked up his beer and offered a toast. "To Nick, survivor of poison, griller of meat, and source of cold wine and beer."

The rest of the gang looked at him with mixed reaction. "What the hell was that?" Georgie asked while the rest laughed.

"I wanted him to know how happy we are that he survived, and we can celebrate with a barbeque and cold beer."

Amber looked at her friends and shrugged. "Don't look at me."

Marie fussed at the table, making sure dishes of home-made potato salad, macaroni salad and coleslaw were full. She also offered steaming corn on the cob as well as a fresh green salad.

"Everything looks great, Marie," Megan said. "Are you sure you don't want to sit down and join us?"

"No, no of course not. I did not agree to come to Misty Manor as a guest. When I stay here, I want to earn my keep."

"Don't be silly," Megan said. "This will probably be one of the last beautiful beach days of the year. Sit outside and enjoy the breeze. Have a glass of wine."

Marie paused for a moment before she moved. "You know, I think I'd enjoy sitting outside for a bit, but I'll skip the wine. I'm not allowed to mix alcohol with my heart pill."

Megan handed her a plate with a napkin and some plastic utensils.

"Thank you," Marie said as she filled the plate with two hot dogs, salad, and an ear of corn. Walking to a rocker in front of the house, she sat down. Dudley and Bella fell to her side, hoping they would be lucky enough to find a dropped morsel to nibble on.

Megan sat at the edge of the picnic table that was placed in the middle of the porch rotunda and took a deep breath of salty ocean air. Looking at the horizon, she watched the waves crash to shore as the seagulls circled the water and cried overhead looking for food.

"What are you looking at?" Nick asked as he sat next to her. His plate was filled with food.

"Just enjoying the ocean and warm air. I still can't believe Misty Manor is all mine, but I do miss Grandma Rose every day. I miss her more as time goes on."

Two years ago, Megan had returned to the Jersey Shore when she lost her job in Detroit. Grandma Rose had been living in the large Grand Victorian Mansion by herself since Hurricane Sandy hit. Grandma Rose needed help, but Megan had been under the impression her father had made arrangements for her. She didn't realize Rose was neglected and dying until she returned to New Jersey. Marie was a longtime family friend and with her help, Megan took care of Rose until she passed. Megan was shocked when she learned she had inherited the beautiful beach home she grew up in as well as most of the Stanford fortune. Misty Manor was hers to preserve, restore to its former glory and enjoy with her friends.

"Penny for your thoughts?" Amber asked as she watched her friend.

Megan shrugged. "Just thinking how lucky I am to be able to sit on this porch with Nick and my good friends by my side. The six of us make quite a team."

"Here, here," Doogie said as he raised his beer. Megan returned the salute with her wine. "Let's eat," Nick said. "After all that cooking, I'm starving."

Megan smiled. "Well, that's a very good sign and I'm glad your plate is full."

The six friends spent the next hour eating and exchanging small talk about Misty Point.

With a loud sigh, Nick sat back and patted his stomach. "I really have to start working out."

"Yes, this is the first summer you've had a pass," Georgie giggled. "I'm used to passing you on my morning run."

Nick frowned. "I'm hoping I'll get back to it next week. The doctor needs to release me so I can get back to my life. And when I do, we'll see who passes whom."

Megan stiffened as Nick spoke those words. She and Marie had taken pains to wait on Nick hand and foot, helping him to heal for six weeks. Megan worried about him and couldn't help feeling hurt at his announcement.

"So, what are your plans then?" Doogie asked as he helped himself to another beer.

Nick shrugged. "I'm not sure yet, but I'll be meeting with Captain Davis. I'll see when I can get back to active duty."

"Well, don't rush," Tommy said. "The crowds are thinning out now that the season is ending. Take your time and build your strength."

"That's my plan for the rest of fall and winter," Nick said. "What does everyone else have planned?"

"I've got a couple of interesting gigs coming up," Tommy said. "Tommy and the Tunes are opening at the Arts Center in a couple weeks."

"I'm proud of my guy," Amber said. "When he really hits it big, I'm going on tour with him."

Tommy rolled his eyes as the group chuckled. "That's going to take a while. What are you doing in the meantime?"

Amber shrugged and pushed her hair back behind her shoulder. "I had a chat with my vice president today. Our corporation is leading a sensitivity training for executive leaders in a couple of weeks. They've asked me to be an ambassador to help host the activities."

"What does that mean?" Georgie asked, frowning at her friend. "What's sensitivity training all about?"

Amber smiled as she spoke. "It's a way to tell an employee they need to start paying attention to their mission and HR policies, without putting them on a formal action plan. This training is aimed at executives and other leaders in the healthcare field. The company gets them together in hopes that spending a week outside of the corporate environment will help them understand the impact of their product. They can return to work with freshened energy and a lot of innovative ideas. But there is a lot of speculation that this is a great way to inspire leaders as well."

"Does that work?" Megan asked as she turned to Amber. "Maybe we should try something similar with the foundation."

"This is the first time I'm going as the ambassador, so I'll let you know when it's over."

"Please do, I'm very interested," Megan said with a smile.

"Not to be rude," Tommy said, "but what exactly does the ambassador do?"

"I'm not sure, but each day the guests have an assignment and I believe we help to make sure they stay on schedule. I'll have more information after the next meeting. What I do know is that they'll be staying at the cabin in the local state park."

"What? North Marsh State Park? Are you sure?" Georgie asked as she chuckled. "They're going to house a bunch of executives in the state park for a week. Why not a fancy hotel?"

"That's the whole point, to get them out of their comfort zone. They'll live in the cabin with no television. There will be zero access to Wi-Fi, computers, or laptops. They won't be able to leave to get their lattes or liquor. No cars are allowed so no restaurant deliveries. They'll be served an old-fashioned dinner around a campfire. No bar, no massages, and no valet." Amber took a sip of her wine and laughed. "It's going to be a hell of a week." Amber could not have known how true her prediction would be.

4

B ob Flowers walked into his office and slammed the door. He
threw himself into his new leather chair and spun to face the
floor to ceiling windows. "How dare they? Sensitivity training, my ass." It was just the sort of corporate circus he had come to
expect with this company. Bob leaned down and pulled out the
bottom side drawer of his desk. Reaching inside, he withdrew a bottle
of Blue Label and a glass. He poured himself two fingers and leaned
back against the plush leather. The smooth amber liquid teased its
way down his throat as he contemplated pouring another.

Without warning, his office door slammed open, and a woman
made her way into the room. She strode to his desk, hitched up her
A-line skirt and sat on the edge. "I hope you saved a glass for me."

Bob shrugged, pulled another glass from the drawer, and filled it
with whiskey while refilling his own. He handed her the glass and
settled back. After a few minutes, he could feel the whiskey flowing
through his veins. He rolled the glass over his forehead and then
looked at the woman. Her glass was already empty. "What else can I
do for you, Ronnie?"

Veronica Lane was a thirty-year-old executive who had worked in
the company for eight years. She had been on a fast track for promo-

tion and Bob wondered whom she had pleased to get to her current position. "What you can do is pour another round and tell me what the hell is going on around here?"

Bob did as he was told. Handing her the glass, he asked, "What do you mean?"

"What is this training camp I'm hearing about?"

Bob shrugged, "Can you believe this crap?"

Veronica raised her whiskey glass toward him, the warm amber liquid starting to take effect. "I heard that you, me, and Alberto are all being sent to some camp. I think they're trying to push us out. That's what this is all about."

"You and Alberto? They're making you go to sensitivity training. Why are they making Alberto go?"

"I don't know," Veronica said, starting to slur her words. "But I'm so mad, I'm putting my resume together tonight."

Bob started to laugh. "If they want us out, that's exactly what they want you to do. You're playing right into their hands."

Veronica frowned as she looked at her whiskey glass. Bob envisioned the glass flying toward his head in the next minute, but to her credit, Veronica held it in her hand. Instead, she took a deep breath, downed the remaining whiskey in one large gulp and slapped the glass onto Bob's desk. "Well, if that's what they want, screw them." She used the back of her hand to wipe her mouth. "I'll go to their little stinky camp. If they're paying my salary for the week, I'll enjoy mother nature and the beach on their dime."

Bob held up his glass and toasted his colleague. "Cheers, that's the spirit. Speaking of which, I'll bring a few bottles to our getaway. That will brighten things up."

Veronica laughed. "It's been a long time since we hid alcohol at summer camp. Who knows, this could be fun, except for Alberto."

Bob waved his free hand toward her. "Alberto's a light weight. Just ignore him and he'll go his own way."

"Let's hope so," she said as she moved to the chair on the opposite side of his desk. As Bob watched, her mouth quivered, and her eyes began to tear up. "I can't believe they're doing this to me. I've worked so hard for this company."

"Maybe that's the problem," Bob said with a toss of his head. "Maybe they don't want initiative, they want you to do what they say, when they say it."

"That's very sad because I have some great ideas," Veronica said.

Bob finished his whiskey and chuckled. "They don't want ideas. They want a great reputation for being a great place to work and they'll tell you what to do so they can get there. In the meantime, I guess the three of us are going to camp."

5

The smell of antiseptic was strong as they entered the hallway. Megan and Nick held hands as they walked down the length of the hospital corridor and stopped at the door of the internist's office.

"Well, here goes," Nick said as he took a deep breath and turned the doorknob to enter the waiting room.

Megan held him back for a moment. "No matter what he says, we'll deal with it. You've been doing great for the last six weeks and you're getting stronger every day."

Nodding, Nick pulled her inside with him and up to the receptionist's desk.

The nurse immediately looked up and addressed them in a hushed tone. "Mr. Taylor?"

"Yes, I'm here for a follow-up." Nick shifted nervously as he waited for her to confirm his appointment.

"Here it is," she said pointing to the screen. "Your appointment is with Dr. Curtis Jeffries. He's running a few minutes behind. Why don't you take a seat?"

"Thanks," Nick said as they headed to the other side of the waiting room and choose two empty seats in the corner.

Nick looked around the room as he shook his leg up and down. Megan reached over and placed a hand on his jean clad thigh to stop him from bouncing his leg. "Calm down, Nick. It will be fine."

He blew out a sigh. "I hate this. I don't like being on this side of healthcare."

"No one does, but you're almost healed."

The side door to the waiting room opened and a med tech leaned out and called Nick's name. Nick and Megan stood up and walked to the door.

"Good morning, Mr. Taylor. We'll be using exam room 3 today." Nick nodded as he followed her to the room. Megan followed silently behind. Nick perched on the edge of the exam table while Megan sat in the side chair. The med tech spent several minutes typing on a keyboard. She then asked several questions and entered the answers into the desk top computer facing the wall. After she finished answering the screening questions, she rose and proceeded to take Nick's vitals.

"Your blood pressure is perfect as well as your oxygen level." Nick watched as she rolled up the sphygmomanometer cuff and placed it back in the holder. "Dr. Jeffries should be in to see you in a few minutes."

"Thank you."

"Have a great day," she said as she left and closed the door behind her.

"Good news already," Megan said as she tried to calm him.

"Let's hope so. Nothing personal but I have to go back to work. I'm going out of my mind."

Several minutes later, they heard a knock on the door. Dr. Curtis Jeffries pushed open the door and walked in with a hearty laugh.

"Nick, my friend, how are you?

Nick nodded. "Good, I'm doing well. What are you doing here? I thought you were in the ER."

"Oh, now the doctors rotate through various clinics a couple times each week, so we stay well rounded. Healthcare is very different than it was years ago."

"That's true," Megan said from over in the corner.

"Miss Stanford. I'm happy that you are not here as a patient today."

Megan smiled. "Believe me, I try to stay as far away from your emergency room as I can."

"I hope so," Dr. Jeffries said. "Every time you work on a mystery, you wind up in my hospital."

"Let's hope it never happens again," Megan said with smile.

Curtis turned to Nick. "So, how are you feeling?"

"Pretty good. I'm ready to go back to work," Nick said hopefully.

Curtis began to laugh. "Driving you crazy, are they?"

"They've been great, but I just can't sit around anymore. I have to do something. How did the tests come out?"

"Everything came out well. Your EKG was normal as was the MRI of your brain. Your kidney ultrasound and lab work all look great. We were lucky to get you into the ER right away and give you immediate treatment for the thallium poisoning. For most patients, it continues to accumulate until it's too late and permanent damage is done."

"As we saw with poor Fiona," Nick said.

"Yes, a tragic result but let's concentrate on you right now. Are you having any lingering symptoms?"

"His hair and eyelashes are coming back nicely," Megan said from the corner.

"I can see that," Curtis laughed as he touched a hand to his own dreads. "How about your chest and legs?"

"My chest has been fine. No cough or pain, but I still have slight numbness in my right foot."

"The poison can certainly cause some nerve damage. In your case, let's hope it resolves completely. Are you exercising?'

Nick shook his head. "No, I was told to wait until after the MRI."

"Well, I think it's about time for you to start walking again. A couple miles a day up and down the boardwalk should start to get you back in shape. Let's not worry about the gym until you walk for a couple of weeks. We can increase the protein in your diet now that we know your kidneys are healed."

"Can I go back to work?"

Dr. Jeffries paused for a few seconds. "I'll talk to Captain Davis about activities. I know you're out on leave, but we can probably return you to light duty. You're not ready to be chasing criminals, but you can certainly help with cases."

Nick nodded. "Thanks."

"I'll talk to Marie about your diet. She'll have you beefed up in no time," Megan offered to make him feel better.

Dr. Jeffries smiled. "It's a start, Nick. Give it a couple of weeks. Take the easy work but use your time to start rebuilding your strength and endurance. When you come back and we see you perform on a treadmill, we'll return you to full duty."

Nick nodded. "You got it, Doc. You'll be here, right?"

Dr. Jeffries shrugged. "I'm not sure, it depends when you get back. Make an appointment now so you're here before Thanksgiving. After that, I'm going back to Jamaica for a well-deserved vacation. Your disability benefits will probably run out by then anyway."

"Sounds good. I'll be back in three weeks. I have to talk to HR and the disability company anyway, although I can't do anything without your report and paperwork."

"Don't you worry. I'll write up my notes and send them in by tonight. You just work on building your strength. We'll both need it to keep Ms. Stanford in line." Curtis smiled as he nodded toward Megan.

Nick couldn't help but chuckle as Megan feigned annoyance. Curtis tilted his head back and let out a deep throaty laugh. He gave Megan a quick hug and tapped the chart against Nick's arm. "I'll see you both soon, but not in my ER."

6

Amber sat at the large mahogany table in the board room. She had arrived early, as she usually did, to give herself a few moments to relax before the presentation took place. Amber was aware the new project would be introduced, and she was asked to be on the team, but she had heard few details up to now.

"Amber, you're here already? Being prompt is an excellent quality." Amber smiled as her boss, Joe Daman, swept into the conference room and placed a folder near his chair at the head of the table. Following behind him was an administrative assistant carrying a large pile of documents. She placed them on the table and passed multiple copies to each side.

The room filled as other coworkers took their place at the table. Waiting for the meeting to begin, the team members greeted each other, discussed the latest weather and their favorite sports team. A few minutes after the hour, Joe Daman, sat in his high-back leather chair and cleared his throat. The room fell silent as the tall, handsome, CEO began to speak.

"Thank you for coming. We're here to discuss a new opportunity for Portal Health. As you know, the corporate world is changing, and it's especially important we have a closer connection with our customers. We are concentrating more on the social determinants of health. The connection between the physical health and the social needs of the community have been well established. We need to spend more time understanding the relationship between our patients and how their experience with education, finance, environment, and availability of food and safety influences their overall health. Healthcare will involve more introspection of the social needs of the patient, their family, and community at large.

"At the same time, healthcare companies need to explore the direct effect of their product on the wellness of patients that use it. To that end, we have been chosen to host a sensitivity training for several executives from the medical field. This program will bring the medical executive into direct contact with patients in several different settings where the exec can directly observe their product at work."

Several of the people around the table nodded as they considered the concept that was being introduced. A gentleman at the far end of the table raised his hand.

"Ray? You have a question?" Joe asked as he gestured toward the man.

"Is this like that television show where they would bring the boss to a workplace as a new employee?"

Joe nodded his response. "Yes, you can think of it exactly that way, except they look for weak points in the company. I guess you could say this new program would do the same for healthcare. The executive can see the direct effect of their product on the patients and the community. It will give healthcare businesses a whole new perspective on what is really needed in the medical community today. The first sessions will be for general executives chosen by their specific company, but once we see what has the most impact, we'll offer a more concise course for higher level leadership."

The members sitting around the conference table looked at each other and started murmuring. A few nodded their heads while they spoke. Joe held his hands up to have everyone quiet down.

"Let's talk about who will be attending the retreat. The first person who was chosen as an ambassador to welcome our guests and guide them through the process is our own Amber Montgomery." Joe turned toward Amber and clapped his hands as the rest of the room joined in. Amber blushed as she heard her boss continue his accolade. "I can't imagine anyone else being a better leader, ambassador, or host than Amber. She'll make the group feel welcome and guide them through some very interesting exercises."

Amber smiled at her boss and nodded her head with gratitude. Joe continued with his announcement. "Amber will also document her impressions as to what makes the most impact on whom so we can continue to tailor this program to be as efficient as possible. In that way, we'll know which activities to expand and which we should drop. She's very intuitive and will be able to see what works the best."

"I'm excited to lead this program," Amber said to her boss, with a smile. "It has great potential for our clients."

"Yes, it does," Joe said as he picked up the folder which sat in front of him. "You all have copies of a report with the names of our guests and the companies they will represent." Joe looked over the table. "Does everyone have a copy? Please let us know if you need one."

Several people raised their hand and the administrative assistant walked over with additional copies of the report.

Amber took the time to quickly thumb through her report to see who she would be hosting.

Joe waited a few moments, then opened his report and began reading. The rest of the team followed suit so they could keep up with the conversation.

"The first three guests will be from Antacus Pharmaceuticals. Antacus is based in Manhattan, NY. They specialize in a variety of medications for general use as well as specific diseases. They are an international company so their product, and therefore patient base, is worldwide. The names of the executives from Antacus are Bob Flowers, Veronica Lane, and Alberto Ortiz. I understand they are all directors, or above, who have been responsible for anything from sales, marketing, and contracts with their product groups and key stakeholders.

"The next company sending an executive is Salacia Medical Supply. Their representative is Felix Cooper. The company delivers medical equipment and durable supplies to patients throughout the state. They're growing rapidly and feel that coaching their leadership will only help them capture a larger part of the market.

"The third company is LPW Medical Records." Joe took a moment to look through his notes until he found a name. "Ah, here it is. They are sending their CIO, Nancy Rogan and another exec, Dante Valentino."

One of the men looked up. "CIO?"

"Chief Information Officer," Joe explained. "The CIO is responsible for computer technologies within a company. Since the beginning of the digital age, every company needs a CIO to oversee the implementation and management of their digital footprint. The larger companies now hire a CTO as well, Chief Technology Officer. Tech is a big part of doing business these days. It also evens the playing field with customers or patients able to reach executives of the companies they work with."

Joe placed the folder on the table. "And that is the reason why they need a company like ours who can help coach executives how to stay relevant to their consumers and guests. It's a changing world out there."

The employees gathered around the table nodded and murmured to each other until Amber asked a question. "Can you give us more details about the training? What are the exact dates and locations? What will each of us be doing?"

"Of course," Joe answered. "Amber, as our ambassador, you will be with our guests for the duration of the conference. It's a front and center position which will reflect the image of our company to help lead, teach, and support. The conference will start a week from Sunday, and you and our guests will all be housed in the main cabin of the local state park. As you know, this arrangement is meant to take everyone out of their comfort zone and away from the technology, gadgets, and the material things we depend on."

Amber shook her head. "It's going to be some week."

Joe nodded. "I agree. It's not an easy position and I expect a few of these leaders will have temper tantrums and throw their entitlement around, but their parent companies have agreed to the terms and feel it will make a significant difference by the end of the week."

"Do we have a schedule yet?"

"Almost," Joe replied. "During their stay, our guests will be visiting local hospitals, nursing homes, attending talks, and educated on how we dispose of medical waste so as not to pollute our ocean and beaches."

"The evening activity will be held around a big bonfire with all meals served in the mess hall. There will be discussion, reflection, and some interesting feedback," Joe said with a chuckle. "The last big night will be Friday night with everyone going home on the weekend."

"Once again, Amber will be front and center and that is where the rest of us will come in. From the office, we'll help support all the travel, food, guides, and needs of the guests."

Joe knocked on the conference table and stood up. "Okay, that's it for now. Next week we'll be busy with prep, and we'll hand out your specific schedules. The next two weeks will be very interesting." He then turned to Amber with a smile. "Let's talk in my private office."

7

"Nick, how are you?" Captain Davis asked as he rounded a desk in the squad room of the Misty Point Police Department. He shook Nick's hand and nodded toward his office.

"Hey, you look happy to see me," Nick said as he walked inside and sat in one of the hard wooden chairs across from the captain's desk.

"I am happy to see you," Davis teased. "We've got a lot of work and it would be a real pain in the ass for me to find and train someone else."

Nick nodded with a grin. "Thanks, I appreciate your concern."

Davis settled himself in his squeaky desk chair, leaned forward and placed his arms on his desk. "Seriously, Nick, how are you? You had me worried there for a while. The doc said this could easily have been fatal if we hadn't called the squad right away."

Looking down at his feet, Nick hesitated. "That's what I'm told since I was sprayed with such a high dose of poison. I'm thankful that Luther and Megan were there."

Davis kept quiet and Nick knew he was holding back his thoughts about Megan Stanford.

"Even if I wasn't involved with her, any responding officer could have suffered the same attack."

"That's true," Davis said. "And she seems like a nice person. I just don't get how she seems to attract so many dead bodies and criminals."

Nick chuckled. "I can't answer that one." Nick flashed Davis a questioning glance. "You talked to the doc?"

"I sure did. He said you were okay for light duty, but you need a little more time to build your strength before you return to a full schedule."

Nick shifted in his chair. "Yes, he has me on a protein diet and starting some endurance training."

Davis nodded. "Good, that's good Nick. I don't want you back here too early, especially if you're handling a gun."

"I get it, Captain, but I'm going stir crazy and I need to do something." Nick sat forward. "You mentioned doing security for that executive training. Is that still available?"

"Technically, yes, but now I'm not sure I should put you on that."

"C'mon, Cap. I'd be babysitting a bunch of executives. What could go wrong?"

Davis raised his eyebrows. "First, I want to know where Megan will be."

"She has nothing to do with this, Cap."

"Are you sure?"

"Of course, I'm sure. But to be honest, I think Amber will be there."

"Amber?"

"You know, Amber Montgomery. She and Georgie Coles are Megan's closest friends."

"I remember," the captain said with a frown. "How is Amber involved?"

"The company she works for, Portal Health, is a healthcare consulting company. I believe they are the host company sponsoring the retreat program. Our group was grabbing a bite to eat a couple of days ago and Amber was discussing the program. I'm not certain it's the same retreat but it sounds likely, especially if it's going to be hosted in the local state park. "

"That sounds like the same one," Davis said while scratching his head.

"C'mon, Cap. Megan has nothing to do with this and Amber is a professional working for her corporation. Megan won't even be present."

"You sure?"

Nick frowned. "Yes, I'm sure. It's not a public event. What are the details? Amber didn't have any information when we met."

Davis scowled as he rooted through papers on his desk. He pulled out a manilla folder, opened it and began to scan the contents. "According to this, Portal Health will be hosting a retreat in the state park starting a week from Sunday. The permit is for approximately one week. Looks like they registered for approximately ten people to stay. Six executives and one company representative, in addition to security and staff." Davis looked up. "I guess Amber is the representative."

"Who are the other people?" Nick asked as he nodded toward the folder.

"Doesn't say specifically. Looks like one spot would be for security and the other for support. I guess they need someone to cook, clean and cater to these people. Maybe they have an open spot in case they send someone else."

"Where is everyone staying?"

Davis read through more of the details. "Everyone will be housed in the main cabin in the park. It's a modern open concept, with luxury bunk beds lining the walls so it's easier for a camp counselor to monitor the crowd. I have no idea how they plan to separate these groups. If I get to choose, security will be housed in the middle of the room. Easier to keep an eye on everyone that way."

"Sounds like a walk in the park," Nick said with a smile. "I'm in."

Davis stared at him for a full minute before Nick tried again.

"Don't make me beg, Cap. How bad can a lot of boring lectures get?"

Davis started laughing. "It depends on whether Megan will be there."

Nick glowered. "I promise Megan will not be at the camp."

Davis tilted his head and tossed the folder over to Nick. "Here, read through this. The retreat starts a week from Sunday and here are all the details they declared on the permit application. That is a courtesy copy, the representatives of North Marsh State Park keep the originals. Officially, we are support if needed. Check with Amber and see if her information matches. She may have the actual agenda for the program. If that's the case, and this is a mighty big if, I want a copy of every detail. You got me, Nick? I want to know exactly when, where and who is going to do what. Is that understood?"

Nick started to grin. "You got it, Cap."

"Make a copy of the file and return the original to my desk before you leave here. And I want the rest of the information before this thing starts."

Standing, Nick grabbed the folder and turned for the door. "Let me go to the copier. I'll have this back to you in a few minutes."

Davis frowned and shook his head. "Why do I feel like this is a bad idea?"

mber walked with her boss toward his private office. When they arrived, he reached for the door and gestured for her to enter. He followed her in and closed the door behind him.

Amber took in the luxurious room. Floor to ceiling windows, wall to wall carpeting, an elegant executive desk, and a large couch. There was a glass coffee table, and two expensive office chairs set up across from it. On the coffee table was a large bouquet of flowers. A small wet bar sat in the corner of the room.

"Please, have a seat," Joe said as he indicated one of the luxury office chairs.

"Your office is stunning," Amber said as she took the chair near the couch.

Joe loosened his tie and hung his suit jacket on a hanger attached to a gold coat rack in the corner.

"Can I get you anything to drink?"

Amber shook her head. "No, I'm fine, thank you."

Joe nodded and sat in the chair opposite to hers. He smiled at Amber and casually crossed his leg as he watched her. "I wanted to discuss this project with you personally."

Amber nodded as she smiled. It didn't escape her that she felt nervous for the first time being alone with Joe.

"Amber, I've been watching you since you joined our company. You're a talented young woman, as well as incredibly beautiful," he added with a shrug.

"Thank you," she said as her face turned crimson. "I've worked hard to meet expectations."

"And that you have," Joe said as he watched her. "Otherwise, we wouldn't be putting you on a project like this."

"Sir?"

He waved his hand at her. "Please, call me Joe. You're part of leadership now. We're all friends."

"Of course, Joe." Amber noticed her hands were trembling slightly. "The project?"

"Yes, this project is very important to our company. If all works out, we'll be on the ground floor of a very new type of leadership coaching. Corporate America is changing. Companies have different and unique needs. Business is digital. Timing is faster. They need to be responsive, and they must have the proper employees to manage their business."

Amber nodded as she listened.

"There are many corporations that will need coaching to lead them in this new world. The average leader will be younger to compete with the digital demands, but they won't have the wisdom or business savvy of a more experienced executive."

"I understand and that does make sense."

Joe continued as he tented his fingers. "That's where our company comes in. We hope to be ahead of the curve, blending the unique digital knowledge of the next generation of leaders with the business savvy of the experienced. This is our first foray into this type of conference so it's important we have the right representative, and that person is you."

Amber wasn't sure if she felt flattered or flustered. "Oh, thank you, Mr. Daman. I mean, Joe."

"This conference will be critical as it will provide important feedback as to the type of services we need to provide, and the pushback we'll receive. We have a blank page and how that gets filled in will all be up to you."

"It sounds like a fantastic opportunity."

"It's not going to be easy. None of these executives are coming voluntarily. They will in the future if we can make the outcome marketable. We need to see how to make it work and put the proper spin on it to sell it to Corporate America."

Amber nodded as she pasted a smile on her face. "There's a bit more to this than I imagined."

"Yes, there is, and a lot is riding on it for the company." Joe smiled as he leaned forward and took her hand. "But there can be a lot of rewards as well. If we do well, the sky is the limit for both of us. I trust you can do this. I know we can do this together."

Amber swallowed when she realized her throat was suddenly dry. As she pulled her hand from his, she said, "I'll do my best. I don't know what to expect when we haven't held a program such as this, yet."

Joe nodded. "You're right, but I'm sure you'll do an excellent job. We'll have a glitch or two."

Amber was thoughtful for a moment. "Remind me who will be helping me with these six executives."

Joe stood up and walked to his desk to consult a group of papers. "Let's see. We hired someone to act as the all-around camp manager if you will. His name is Phil Beckman.

"What will his duties be?"

"He'll do the cooking and prepare meals, wash dishes, oversee the bonfire, and help with house issues. He may be bringing someone with him. We signed a contract for one week of services. You're our ambassador. Your duties are to help the guests organize and alert them to their talks and assignment for the day. You'll keep them on schedule and travel with them to all events."

"How will they be getting to their assignment?"

"We have someone driving a small bus for travel," Joe mused. "We may have the manager responsible for that. I'll have to check, but they can't drive themselves as there are no cars allowed. That way, we'll know they're not able to connect with Wi-Fi or go shopping."

Amber raised her eyebrows. "And if they insist or simply leave the premises?"

"Well, it is a retreat, not a prison. If they leave, we'll inform their company, and they are the responsible party." Joe walked over to Amber and wrapped an arm around her waist. "Don't worry, I'll be dropping by to help explain the week's activities and to support you. Also, we hired security which will be provided by the local Misty Point Police Department."

Amber nodded and silently prayed that Nick got his boss to let him take the assignment.

9

The boardwalk was lit up at night, even though it was October. A few of the shops were open for coffee, pastry, ice cream, and pizza, but most of the summer venues were now closed. The Misty Point Police Department continued to patrol the area so there was minimal crime or drug distribution, which kept it safe for residents staying in nearby hotels or those who enjoyed their evening walks. Once the weather turned cold, the remaining shops would close until spring.

"You're doing well," Megan said as she walked with Nick. "Our pace is around 16 minutes per mile. How's your leg?" Megan had noticed a small limp when Nick tried to pick up his speed, but he pushed so he could strengthen as quickly as possible.

"It's okay."

"You don't sound very convincing." Megan tried to side eye his gait but wasn't very successful.

"It doesn't matter. I have to keep going. Part of my leg and foot are numb. What I feel are tingles. Lots of tingles and my toes are numb, but the doc said those things may go away once I start walking and go to physical therapy."

"This boardwalk is two miles long," Megan said. "It will be easy to walk several different routes to increase your milage. We just have to make sure you don't overdo it in the beginning and injure yourself. I know you're eager, but things take time."

"I'm out of time," Nick said, his frustration showing in his voice. "I think I can manage a daily walk."

Megan tried to lighten the conversation. "Walking daily will help me as well. I used to love getting up every morning and walking two miles along the boardwalk. I'm glad to get back to that routine."

"Okay, we'll walk for now," Nick said as he nodded his head. "But in a couple of weeks, I'll be running with Georgie in the morning. My pace will be slow when I start but I can build up."

Megan wrapped her hand around Nick's arm. "I know you will. You're on the road to recovery."

Nick squeezed her hand as they walked. He then pointed down the boardwalk. "Hey, there's Amber."

"She called earlier and said she would have a table and coffee waiting for us," Megan said as she waved to let her friend know they saw her. Amber waved back and then turned when a server appeared at her side with a food tray. Several items were placed on the outdoor wooden table and the server went back inside the restaurant.

Amber sipped her coffee as she waited for her friends to approach. "Hey, save some for us," Megan teased as they neared the table.

"There's plenty to go around." Amber waved her arm toward the table. "Pull up a seat."

"Don't mind if I do," Nick said as he pulled out a bench and sat down. Amber handed him a plate and pushed the tray of half sandwiches and dessert in his direction.

"This looks great," Megan said as she poured two cups of coffee.

"Nothing but the best for my good friends," Amber said with a smile.

Nick stopped what he was doing, food halfway to his mouth. "Why don't I like the sound of that?" He looked back and forth between Megan and Amber. Megan shrugged and they both looked toward Amber who immediately placed her hand on Nick's arm.

"Nick, I need you."

"Excuse me?" Megan asked with a grin.

"I need Nick's services," Amber tried again.

Nick shoved a pastry into his mouth. "I like where this is going, so far."

Megan punched him in the shoulder before she turned to her friend. "Out with it and get right to the point. What's going on?"

Amber gave a lopsided smile and looked at her friends. "We had a meeting today at work about the retreat."

"And?" Megan asked as she choose a sandwich.

"I think I'm in over my head. My boss, Joe Daman, spoke about this retreat at a staff meeting and explained its importance to the future of our company, and it involves more than I imagined. Plus, it sounds like the so-called guests are going to be miserable."

Nick finished chewing and was thoughtful for a moment. "How can I help you?"

Amber grabbed his forearm. "First, please tell me that you're the police officer they assigned to this project. Please, please, oh please."

"Will you be in the North Marsh State Park, starting next Sunday?"

"Yes, we are," Amber said, her smile turning wide.

"Then no, that's not me," Nick said as he took a bite of a sandwich. He couldn't help laughing when he saw her face fall.

"Megan, your boyfriend is a jerk," Amber said with a frown.

"I'm sorry. I couldn't resist." Nick grabbed her hand. "Yes, I've convinced Captain Davis to let me take the detail, so I will be there."

"Oh, thank you. I am so happy to hear you say that." Amber launched herself to hug him around the shoulders while Megan looked on curiously.

"I'm glad you two are so happy to be together, but is there a specific reason other than Nick's natural charm that's making you this ecstatic?"

"Yes, several. First, I found out we're all in one cabin. There are six executive guests, a camp manager and us." Amber looked at Nick and continued her story. "The cabin is one large room with a desk in the middle."

"Which is mine," Nick broke in.

"What? I was going to sit there," Amber pouted.

"No, I can't keep an eye on the whole cabin if I'm stuck on one side. How many guests will you have on each side?

Amber shrugged. "All I know is there will be ten people in a cabin that sleeps eighteen. The bunks are built into the walls. The rest depends on who feels comfortable sleeping on each side."

"Which is exactly why I need to be in the middle so I can keep an eye on both sides."

Amber's eyes pleaded with Megan. "Please, let me stay with your boyfriend."

Nick burst out laughing and spilled coffee on the table. "Whoa, Amber. I like you as a friend, but I have committed to Megan."

Amber's stare cut into him. "Hold your horses, big guy. I don't want to *sleep* with you, I just want to stay in the same section as you."

"For five nights?" Nick asked with a smug grin.

"Yes, although I warn you, I probably won't be getting a lot of sleep. This whole thing is making me anxious. Plus, my boss says he's going to stop by to help."

"Does he make you nervous?" Nick asked, picking up a strange vibe.

"Hey, can we join you?"

The trio looked up to see Georgie, Doogie and Tommy approach the table. Tommy sat next to Amber and immediately pulled her to him. "What's going on?"

Megan started to laugh and said, "Well, Amber was just asking me if she could sleep with Nick."

"What the hell?" Tommy said as he looked at his girlfriend.

Amber frowned at Megan and turned back to Tommy. "I would never sleep with him."

"Hey," Nick pretended to be wounded as the rest of the table started laughing.

They helped themselves to coffee and food and listened to Amber explain the retreat. She described the guests, their involuntary status, the proposed activities, and the cabin arrangements. "I'm happy Nick will be with me all week because I have a feeling this assignment will suck."

"I'd be more than happy to serve as a bodyguard," Tommy said. "Except that I'm on the docks during the day and we have a gig on Friday night, so I'll let Nick guard you as long as he doesn't touch you."

Nick held up his hand. "You have my word, Tommy. Besides, I have a feeling there's not going to be time to relax. In my experience, downtime at these types of retreats turns into trouble. I probably won't even be in the room at night if I'm doing rounds or something," Nick said with a serious expression. "Problem is, I hope I don't have to chase down these guests."

"That's why they keep everyone together," Amber explained. "No one can go off and drink or do whatever."

"And I'm sure they'll all follow the rules," Nick said sarcastically.

Amber shook her head. "I have no idea what to expect. I'm just happy to hear I'm not going to be alone with these people. I'm hoping it will go well, and we'll all be one happy family at the end of the week, but you know the best laid plans and all."

"I guess we'll find out," Nick said as he passed the food tray around the table and then popped another miniature pastry in his mouth. "Here's to meeting you in the parking lot on Sunday morning."

10

"Do you have all your bags?" Megan asked as they walked toward the car.

Nick nodded as he put the grey canvas duffel in the back seat. "That's all I need. I'd leave extra clothes in my car, but I don't want my Camaro sitting in the parking lot of the state park all week."

"I don't blame you," Megan said. "Besides, it will give me an excuse to drive fresh clothes and food over to you during the week."

Nick laughed as he pulled Megan to his chest and kissed the top of her head. "Thank you for understanding that I have to do this."

Megan turned her head and rested her face against his chest. Hugging him tightly, she said, "I hope this assignment brings you back to you." She pulled back and looked up into his eyes. "I want you to feel better, stronger and more confidant, but above all, I want you to be safe. I don't ever want to feel the way I did when you were in that emergency room."

Nick leaned down and captured her mouth with his. "I'm sorry if I was a pain in the butt. You did an excellent job taking care of me and I wasn't very gracious about it."

"Hmmn, Officer Nick Taylor. You'll miss me when you're lying in a cold cabin, praying for a hot shower, delicious meal, and a decent night's sleep."

Nick laughed as he opened the driver's door. "I'm sure I will."

The pair put on their seatbelts before Nick pulled out of the driveway and headed for town. They stopped at a local bakery and picked up several cups of coffee, a box of donuts and drove toward the state park.

Fifteen minutes later, Nick slowed as his car reached the paved road leading into North Marsh State Park. They passed the brown wooden gate as they entered and drove until they reached the parking area. Nick chose a spot, in the corner near the path that led to the cabin and backed his car into the space. Looking at his watch, he said, "We've got two hours before the so-called guests arrive. C'mon, let's go stow my bag in the cabin. I want to check it out before everyone arrives."

The pair got out of the car. Megan held her coffee as Nick pulled his things out of the back. As they reached the path, they stopped at a brown wooden sign which held a posting board behind clear plastic. On display were hiking maps of the area. Megan studied them as she sipped her coffee. She then read aloud.

"The red trail is approximately a mile long and will lead to the marsh. Natural wildlife and beautiful scenery can be enjoyed as you walk. The green trail is approximately two miles long and will end in the bird observatory. Here, you will find some of the best birding and wildlife locations within the state. The blue trail is approximately a mile long and leads to the beautiful sandy beaches of New Jersey. Weekly guided walks and other programs are led by our Associate Naturalists who will provide extended opportunities to view the natural wonders of the area. Sign up and tour times are listed inside the office."

Megan turned to Nick as they proceeded down the path. "Those hikes sound intriguing. We should come back and try one sometime."

"How about in the spring? I don't think the park holds those tours after Labor Day but while I'm here I'll check into whether they staff the office during the winter."

"I must admit I've never spent a lot of time in the state park. I'm curious about it."

"I'm curious about the cabin and what's going to happen over the next week," Nick said as he hoisted his duffel over his shoulder. "There it is." He pointed toward a building half hidden behind a grove of trees.

"It's bigger than I thought."

"It's big enough to sleep eighteen people." As the path curved, he pointed to the right. "That must be the main building. This place has a mess hall with wooden tables, benches, and a commercial kitchen. There is a recreational hall, restrooms with showers, and activities in the natural wilderness, including sporting events, and fireplaces both inside the building and out back."

"I'm sure the campfires will be very welcome, now that it's October," Megan said with a smile. "Do you get to lead the group in song?"

Nick turned toward Megan with a frown on his face. "I'll leave that to Amber."

Megan giggled. "Nick, I'm trying to lighten your mood. Everything will be fine. Please try to relax. You never know, I've heard these excursions are very enjoyable. It may not be as luxurious a facility as they're used to, but many people purposely escape the city life to live in nature for a while. You know, get off the grid. I'm sure that's exactly why these companies chose this sort of retreat."

Nick shrugged. "I'll guess we'll find out at the end of the week. Let's stop in the cabin first."

The pair turned into the dirt path and climbed the six wooden steps that led up to the cabin. The screen door squeaked as Nick opened it up. They pushed past the heavy wooden inner door and into the cabin.

"This looks very nice," Megan said as she looked around the large room. She saw numerous couches and chairs near the center of the room. On the far wall was a large fireplace and next to it sat a heavy-duty steel firewood rack filled with cut and stacked logs. A smaller box held precut kindling.

Nick walked straight ahead. He eyed the bunks on both sides of the room. The middle led to a small area on the far wall which held a camp counselor's desk. In the corner was a small room which housed a toilet and sink.

"This is beautiful," Megan said as she peered around the room. "I love the open design, especially if you had a younger group. The wood is gorgeous. Where are the showers?"

"In the restrooms. It's a separate building down the path."

"Oh, very interesting. Everything looks clean. The beds are crisp, and the floor is spotless."

"It's a very nice cabin. Enough to immerse you in the wilderness but safe, warm, and clean. This set up will make my life a lot easier if everyone behaves."

"Hello? Is someone in here?"

Nick and Megan turned when they heard the female voice.

"Hey, I'm glad it's you two," Amber said as she found her friends.

"I was just admiring the cabin," Megan said as she turned toward Amber. "It looks great and like there's been maid service. The beds appear to be made up."

"Yes, for this group, we had a service come in with clean linens, comforters, and pillows. The guests are welcomed to bring and use any personal items they want but it's not necessary."

"It's looks like this could be a lot of fun," Megan said.

"As long as everyone is good with being off the grid and back to nature," Amber said with a shrug. She turned to Nick. "I looked at the counselor's area. The two beds nearest the desk are for chaperones and counselors. I put my bag on one of the beds. Are you good with that?"

Nick shrugged. "I'm okay with it as long as you are."

"We'll find out," Amber said with a laugh as she turned to Megan.

Megan shook her head as she sipped her coffee.

"What are you two doing here so early?" Amber asked. "I had to come and make sure the hospitality service did everything we asked, and I have to go check the kitchen or rather mess hall next."

"I wanted to scope it all out," Nick said. "Better to stake our ground and see what we have to work with before everyone else arrives."

"I get it. They should be here in about 90 minutes. After they have some time to stow their stuff, we'll meet in the common area and get to know everyone. I'll give them a schedule."

"Sounds like a plan," Nick said as he walked to the counselor's desk. He put his duffel on the unoccupied bed and turned to survey the room.

"What's up?" Amber asked as she and Megan watched him.

"Just strategizing what will work best during the night. If you don't mind, I'd like to sleep on this side of the desk. I'll probably be up patrolling part of the night or sitting at the desk reading. Early morning, I'll be able to get some sleep once you all go off on your assignments."

Amber nodded. "I didn't even think of that. Sure, take whatever area you want."

"Appreciate it," Nick said with a tight nod.

"I've got to get to the kitchen," Amber said as she looked at her watch. "I'm so glad you're here, Nick. I'd be nervous as hell if I were here alone."

"I'm sure you'll all be fine," Megan said, aware that Nick was more edgy than usual. "Amber, I'm always available to come help out if you need me."

"I'd love that, but we're not supposed to have anyone here that isn't connected to the project. You know, insurance, liability, all the fun corporate reasons."

Megan nodded. "I get it. Just offering."

Amber gave her friend a hug and headed out the screen door. As they watched Amber leave the cabin, Megan reached for Nick's hand. "You seem a little uptight. I'm sure all will go well."

Nick took a deep breath. "I guess I'm worried about going back to work. What if I don't have the endurance? I need to get through this."

"You'll work it out and I'm sure the police department has someone to relieve you, if necessary. You also will have someone from the park available, right? They can't expect you to be on duty 24/7 for the whole week."

Nick swallowed as he nodded. "There are resources but I'm hoping not to use them. I'm not sure if anyone is on the grounds. The NJ State Park Police Department is available 24/7 if I need them, but I want to prove that I'm ready and able to be back full time."

Nick turned and pulled Megan into a tight hug. He leaned his head forward and kissed her deeply. When he pulled back, he held his forehead to hers and whispered. "I know I haven't been an easy patient and haven't been as appreciative as I should be. I do want you to know how much I love you and how much I appreciate everything you've done for me. I couldn't have recovered nearly as fast if it wasn't for you."

Megan hugged him tighter and leaned in for another kiss. "Just get this week over with and come back to me." Her grin was mischievous. "When you're fully healed, I've got some more specific positions in mind for you."

Nick laughed. "Now that I'll look forward to." He gently kissed her again and pulled her by the hand. "C'mon, let's go back to the car and finish our breakfast. I want to watch the guests arrive and get a sense of what we'll be dealing with for the rest of the week."

Megan teased as they walked. "Nick Taylor, camp counselor. Really, how hard can this be?"

11

Ten minutes later, Nick and Megan settled into their seats and opened the donuts. Megan placed her coffee cup in the holder and plucked a chocolate cream donut out of the box. "I haven't had one of these in years." She took a bite and then brushed at the white powder on her face. "I'm going to have to walk an extra two miles today, but this is worth it."

Nick sipped his coffee and watched as a black suburban pulled into the parking lot. It pulled to a stop in front of a low wall of wooden logs blocking access to cars past the macadam.

"I'm glad we got here early. If these are the first guests, they're early as well."

"I can't imagine anyone else arriving at a state park in a black SUV limousine," Megan said as she finished her treat.

They watched as a driver exited the vehicle and opened the back passenger doors. Two people appeared from the back seat and Nick watched with interest as they stretched and looked around the parking lot. He grabbed his file and started to read names and profiles. "There are only two women. One is Veronica Lane from Antacus Pharmaceuticals, and the other is Nancy Rogan from LPW Medical Records. Veronica is from Manhattan, NY and Nancy is the

Chief Information Officer working with computers in NJ. I don't want to profile but I'm going to guess this woman is Veronica Lane."

Megan turned to Nick. "Why would you say that?"

"Several reasons," Nick replied as he began to count with his fingers. "According to the file, Veronica is younger, and works for a large pharmaceutical company in the city. It makes sense they would send their executives in a limo which happens to have a NY license plate. She's wearing a lot of makeup and has her hair styled which is not what we would normally see when someone visits a state park. So, I'm guessing Manhattan here."

"Interesting," Megan said as she nodded.

"There are two men registered from that company, Bob Flowers, and Alberto Ortiz. Only one man in the car. Why wouldn't they have all their executives together?"

"Many reasons. They may live in completely different directions. Maybe one dropped out," Megan shrugged. "I'm sure you'll find out, but I can tell you, these two people do not look happy."

"No, they don't."

They watched as the driver opened the trunk of the SUV and retrieved a pile of expensive luggage. He then pulled out a foldable cart and stacked the bags on it. After looking around to establish their location, the trio began to walk up the path toward the cabin.

"That's the face people make when they suck on sour lemons," Megan said with a smile as Nick nodded his agreement.

"I'm sure they'll be a fun addition to the group."

A short time later another car arrived, and another man and woman exited. Nick spoke as he pointed with his coffee cup. "I'll bet that is Nancy Rogan and Dante Valentino from LPW Medical Records." Again, their driver popped the trunk open, but the pair retrieved their own bags. The woman, dressed in casual slacks and a light sweater, pulled the handle out of her case, and began to tow the luggage behind her. Her partner pulled a sleek carry bag from the car, and both walked up the path toward the cabin as the driver turned and sped away.

"That's four guests and we have another forty minutes until the party officially gets started," Nick said as he looked at his watch. "I guess I should get up to the cabin and see what I can do to help Amber."

"Okay, I'll go then. I can't believe you're going to let me drive this baby blue Camaro home," Megan teased.

"I hope you realize this is the first time I have ever let anyone drive my car and I trust you'll take care of it."

"Of course, just as soon as I get a little joyride in." Megan opened her door, got out of the car, and made her way toward the driver's side.

Nick slid out from behind the steering wheel and pulled her into a hug. He looked worried when he let her go.

"You remind me of a homesick teen going off to summer camp for the first time," she teased. "It will all be fine, Nick. Once you get through this assignment, you'll know if you're ready to get back to work full time."

"I know," he nodded. "You'll come if I call or send a message?"

"I'll be here in a heartbeat. I know you don't have great Wi-Fi but I'm sure they have a regular phone line you can use if you need to. This may be against the rules, but I was planning on popping in time to time to check on you anyway. I may not be allowed to attend the retreat, but the state park is still open to the public and I doubt they'll arrest me if I happen to leave some treats behind."

"I appreciate that," Nick smiled. "We have an emergency key to the park office, and they have a landline there if we need it." He hugged her once again and watched as she got behind the wheel and adjusted her seat. Starting the car, she opened the window to say goodbye and he leaned in on the door. "Seriously, take good care of my car."

Shaking her head, she laughed, put the car in gear and drove off. Checking the rearview mirror, she choked up as she watched Nick wave after her from the parking lot.

12

Nick walked up to the cabin and stepped inside to find the first four guests in the front area with luggage on the floor. They looked around, lost as to what they should be doing. Amber had not returned from the kitchen, not expecting them to arrive as early as they did.

"Welcome," Nick said. "You're all a few minutes early. Amber should be in to greet you very shortly. Just have a seat and relax."

They moved toward the couches and chairs, some grumbling under their breath. Veronica leaned forward with distaste and brushed off the chair before she sat hoping there was no mold in the cushion.

Nick shook his head and headed toward the back center of the room. Within ten minutes, two more gentlemen walked in with their bags. "Welcome gentleman, find a seat. Amber should be with us momentarily."

They did as they were asked. The group started to get restless and pulled out cell phones. Bob Flowers looked at Veronica. "You have any reception?"

"Not a damn thing," she said as she threw her phone back into her purse.

Amber rushed into the room and threw a thankful glance at Nick when she saw him sitting with the group. She took a deep breath, pulled herself up to her full height and addressed the guest executives.

"Hello, welcome everyone. I'm sorry I wasn't here to greet you, but I see Nick has things well in hand. My name is Amber Montgomery and I work for Portal Health. I'll be your ambassador over the coming week." Amber waited for a few seconds to allow the group to respond but instead was met with total silence. "We'll talk more about the agenda later, but I'd like everyone to introduce yourself, so we know who's here." Amber looked to the left and pointed to the first gentleman. "Let's start with you. Can you tell us your name and the company you're representing?"

After clearing his throat once or twice, a very tanned gentleman with a slight accent addressed the small crowd. "Hello. My name is Dante Valentino. I am a manager for LPW Medical Records. Thank you very much."

"Welcome, Dante." When he nodded, Amber looked at the next person and smiled for encouragement.

The woman stood up. "Nancy Rogan, CIO of LPW Medical Records." She gave a half wave and sat down.

"Welcome, Nancy," Amber said as she looked at the next person.

"Bob Flowers from Antacus Pharmaceuticals in Manhattan." He waved from his seat, offered a lopsided grin and a nod.

"Welcome, Bob."

The next woman stood up and smoothed her designer pants. She started speaking in a sultry voice. "Hi, my name is Veronica Lane. I also work at Antacus Pharmaceuticals."

"Welcome, Veronica," Amber said as she continued to address each executive.

"Hi, my name is Felix Cooper," the next guest said as he looked around the room. He paused for a few seconds and then continued, "I work for Salacia Medical Supply in New Jersey. I'm happy to be here and meet all of you for the first time."

Amber smiled. "Thank you, Felix. We're happy to meet you as

well." She then turned to the last member and said, "We always save the best for last?"

A Hispanic gentleman nodded. "My name is Alberto Ortiz. I know several of these guests. I am from Antacus Pharmaceuticals."

"Thank you, Alberto, and welcome." Amber then clasped her hands in front of her.

"We have an interesting schedule for you this week and we'll go over all of that later. For now, I'd like everyone to choose a bunk. We're all in this one, big, happy room. Locate a bunk, stow your gear, and then come back so we can go over the necessities like food and showers." She then walked toward the back of the common room so she could speak with Nick as the group slowly stood up, grabbed their bags, and walked toward the walls.

"What do you think?" Amber asked quietly as she sat with Nick and watched the guests choose their bunks.

Nick crossed his arms. "Well, no one looks thrilled to be here. It's interesting how they're measuring each other up and deciding who to sleep near at night."

Amber nodded. "I was wondering if they would cluster by company or gender, but it appears they are pairing up with coworkers. Although it's odd that Bob and Veronica from the drug company are separated from their coworker, Alberto."

"Yes, I can see he's chosen an isolated space, distant from the others."

"Maybe he has social anxiety disorder or just doesn't like being near others when he sleeps."

"Coworkers don't always work in the same department or like each other," Nick pointed out.

"That's true," Amber agreed. "There were quite a few people at our board meeting I've never met." Amber sighed and then look at Nick. "That Felix seemed a bit creepy."

Nick silently nodded. "It's interesting when you throw different personalities together. We'll see how this works out."

13

M egan cruised toward the ocean in Nick's Camaro. She hoped all went well this week, and he was able to gain strength and endurance. She was frightened when he was first poisoned, afraid he would die. Thankfully, the first antidote, given within hours of his exposure, stopped the deadly progression of the poison.

Megan pulled into one of the parking spots facing the ocean. The summer crowd had retreated and there were plenty of free spots open. She climbed out of the car and walked toward one of the benches. Sitting for a moment, she allowed herself to breathe, find some balance and calm down. Everything had happened so quickly in the last year. Grandma Rose's death, reconnecting with Nick and friends, her inheritance, taking ownership of Misty Manor, chairing her grandmother's foundation and the committees it supported.

She never expected to fall in love with Nick and hope for a future together. A future that he would never accept if it was handed to him. He was working hard to return to work, to good health and feel worthy in her eyes. Megan wished this week was a big step forward with his plan.

"You're not considering drowning yourself, are you?"

The man's voice jarred Megan from her reverie. "Luther? You scared me."

Luther laughed and joined her on the bench. "Didn't expect to meet you here. An army could have snuck up on you. You looked like you were a million miles away."

Megan shrugged. "I guess I was. I'm just worried about Nick."

"Is something new going on? I thought he was doing well."

Megan slowly nodded. "He is, thanks to you. He was lucky you were there for him that night." Luther Tucker was an old friend of Nick's. She knew he was a former black-ops agent who now handled private security. Beyond that, Megan had no idea when he and Nick had met and what experience they had together.

The night Nick was poisoned, Luther stopped her from touching Nick, and managed to restrain the culprit until the police and ambulance arrived.

"As I recall, we were both there," Luther said, "but I'm there for him whenever he needs me. I owe him that and more but that's a long story."

Megan laughed. "Not everyone is lucky enough to have a friend with experience in special ops. If I haven't thanked you, I want to do it again."

"We've covered that in full. What's going on now that has you so upset?"

"You know Nick has been getting restless. He went to Dr. Jeffries who gave him clearance for light duty. He talked Captain Davis into giving him a special assignment. I don't know if you remember Amber, my friend who works for Portal Health?"

"I remember her," Luther said as he nodded for Megan to continue.

"Her company is hosting a retreat for executives in the state park, and they hired Nick as a private security guard for the week. They're all staying in the main cabin and must go to various activities each day. Nick thinks it'll be an easy assignment, but these executives are not all there by desire. I think it's a mandatory assignment for some."

"Grown adults better behave," Luther said as he adjusted the hat around his head.

"I'm sure they will. I'm hoping Nick does well and gets his confidence back."

"Want me to call him? Check on the guy?"

Megan shook her head. "You can't. There's no service in that part of the park. That's why they chose that cabin. They've purposely removed the distractions that cell phones and technology provide."

Luther smiled and winked. "Well then it sounds like my runs for the next couple of days are going to take place in the state park. Got to stay in shape and there's no law as to where I can run."

"Would you? I mean could you do that? It would mean the world to me if he had someone keep an eye on him. It can't be me. He already thinks I mother him too much."

Luther started laughing. "Sure, I'll be happy to do that."

"What's so funny?" Megan asked as she watched him.

"To be honest, he told me he'd be away and asked me to keep an eye on you."

14

"Let's gather by the fireplace," Amber said as she called out to the group and made sure the furniture was circled nearby. Slowly, the small group reassembled and picked various chairs and couches to lounge in. Nick stayed in the background with his arms crossed and watched them gather.

Amber stood in front, clutching her hands before her as she nervously welcomed them to the cabin. "Once again, I want to welcome you all to the Portal Health Retreat. We have a lot of activities planned for you this week, but we also want to give you time to relax and adjust to our beautiful location."

Amber watched as Bob Flowers continued to work with his cell phone, obviously more frustrated by the moment. "Does this paradise have any Wi-Fi?"

"Well, no. That's one of the parameters of this retreat," Amber said as she heard a chorus of moans and complaints. "The point is to remove technology from our environment and concentrate on our customers, the patients and families we serve with our products."

"This arrangement stinks," Bob said as he threw his phone on the couch. "What the heck are we supposed to do all week."

"That's what I'd like to discuss," Amber said with a shaky smile as she looked at Nick in the back of the room. He was about to walk to her side when they heard another male voice break in.

"Why don't we give our ambassador a chance to answer the first question before we throw others at her."

Amber turned to see her boss, Joe Daman, walk into the room. He was dressed in expensive outdoor gear and carried the air of success despite not being in a large conference room in a three-piece suit. Amber was amazed to realize his ability to combine fashion with function for the retreat.

"Mr. Daman?" Amber stepped back to allow him the center of the room, but he gently guided her to stand next to him. She turned toward the guests. "I'd like to introduce the President and CEO of Portal Health, Mr. Joe Daman."

After a low energy welcome, Joe began to speak. "Welcome to North Marsh State Park and the Portal Health Retreat. I realize this is new to most, if not all of you, but we've designed a unique week for you to reconnect your product with your customer. The world is changing and it's time for industries and corporations to think outside the box. To move away from the typical structure and flex with your customers' needs." He smiled as he continued to charm the group in front of him and Amber noticed several of the guests begin to nod and smile.

"We have designed a transformational week to take you away from the day-to-day grind and reconnect your ability to achieve personal growth and empowerment while enjoying nature. As you know, being in nature is the new therapy to eradicate fatigue, brain fog and enhance our wellness. We will then teach you ways to keep that spirit alive as you return to your business world free of burn-out, fatigue and assumptions about your customers."

Joe turned and placed his arm around Amber's shoulders. "Amber is our ambassador for the inaugural retreat in this beautiful state park. She will fill you in on the details of the conversations and activities we have planned for you this week. You will be rejuvenated, relaxed, and restored as you make your transformative journey."

Joe turned and nodded at Amber as he stepped back toward the fireplace. Amber turned toward the group, feeling empowered herself. "Thank you, Mr. Daman. I'd like to take a moment to orient you to the grounds, facilities, and recreational aspects of the state park. We will hold our presentations and conversations in various places to fully enjoy all the flora and fauna we can find."

"As long as we don't catch a parasite or poison ivy," someone murmured as the others snickered. Amber looked up but couldn't identify who had spoken.

"I assure you the state park is as clean as it is beautiful. There are trails that lead to the ocean as well as the marsh, bogs, and other beautiful hiking destinations. In addition, each day we will have a trip to either a hospital, nursing home or the beach where we will have a medical lecture and orientation to relevance." Amber searched the crowd and noticed they were antsy. "The next hike I'd like to offer is the one to the mess hall so we can all have some lunch. I'll distribute maps of the state park while we're eating. Once we're done, you'll have free time to explore the area. We don't have Wi-Fi, fast foods, or liquor stores for miles around, so your phones won't work. That means no calls for pizza delivery." Several people started to snicker. "While you're eating, I'll post a schedule of events for the week. You have free time between lunch and dinner to explore the state park and relax before dinner. After dinner, we'll have an outdoor bonfire and get to know each other better. Then a great night's sleep, breakfast and our first presentation in the morning."

Veronica raised her hand. "This may sound a bit indelicate, but can we start our mystery tour with the bathrooms?" When the others nodded and chimed in, Amber smiled and gestured toward the wooden screen door.

"Of course, let's move on to tour the bathrooms and showers."

As the group stood and moved toward the door, Amber looked back at Nick and rolled her eyes.

She herded the group outside but was stopped and pulled aside on the porch by Joe Daman. "Amber, you're doing a fantastic job. I know this feels like babysitting a group of campers, but it will get better once they shake off the corporate dust. Just stay strong and don't let them get the better of you. Be the camp counselor from hell."

Amber started to laugh. "I will certainly try, Mr. Daman."

He smiled and held her hand a fraction too long. "Please, call me Joe."

Amber blushed as she nodded. Her boss suddenly dropped her hand when Nick moved through the screen door and started to introduce himself. "Nick Taylor, Misty Point Police Department. I'm your security for the week."

Nick and Joe Daman watched as Amber scurried down the steps and led the group toward the wooden building where the showers and bathrooms were located.

"How do you do, Nick? Thank you for being with us this week," Joe said as he shook Nick's hand. "What do you think of the group?"

Nick gestured toward the bathrooms with his chin. "I don't know. Some of them don't look happy to be here."

"The inaugural event is always the hardest. We're hoping the retreat is successful and the benefit becomes obvious. Maybe we'll have a waiting list and can run this retreat several times each year."

Nick shrugged as he answered. "I guess only time will tell."

"At any rate, I imagine this assignment shouldn't be too stressful for you."

Nick immediately stiffened. "Why do you say that?"

"No reflection on you, of course. This group may not be thrilled but at least they're not hardened criminals." Joe then tapped Nick on his upper arm and walked down the wooden stairs as he whistled.

15

Megan parked the Camaro on the side of the driveway, away from any activity. She didn't want Nick to return to find his beloved car scratched or damaged. She made her way to the front door and was greeted by her group of fur babies. Her cat Smokey, and two dogs, Dudley and Nick's new adoption, Bella. The dogs jumped in front of her while Smokey hung in the background of the foyer. "Okay, okay. I gather you all would like to go out." Megan opened the door, and the dogs went running for the weeds next to the beach.

"Megan, is that you?" Marie popped into the foyer from the kitchen.

"Yes, I just got back from dropping Nick off at the state park." Megan watched as the dogs chased each other in circles while Smokey took the opportunity to brush up against her legs.

"How did it go? The weather looks beautiful."

"I think they're all a little nervous, but we'll see," Megan answered as she continued to watch the pets.

"In the meantime, what would you want for dinner?"

Megan turned to face her. "Marie, why don't you take the night off? You've been cooking up a storm for a month to nurse Nick back to health."

"And loved every minute of it," Marie said. "The kitchen is my happy place."

Megan laughed as she hugged her friend. "Georgie will be over any minute now. We must talk about the drive for the food pantry. Pastor Lee wants to meet with us tomorrow to talk about our plans and I thought we should make some before we go there."

"Well, then maybe just a pizza tonight?"

"That sounds fabulous. Let's order from Antonio's. They can deliver while we talk about the food pantry."

"We?" Marie asked with a smile.

"Of course, we. Who better to organize the food drive than you? We'll all help but you would be fabulous as the organizer here. I can barely tell one spice from another."

"Megan, I would love that," Marie said, her smile even wider. "Let me put on a pot of coffee and I just made some fresh cinnamon scones we can nosh on while we talk."

"Sounds great to me. I'll get some pads and pens, but first I must let the dogs back in the house. We'll meet in the kitchen as soon as Georgie gets here."

"Let me get started and thank you, Megan. I'm thrilled to help with this."

"I knew you would be," Megan laughed and turned to find the dogs.

16

Nick walked into the mess hall to find Amber and the group lined up against the far wall. Past the wall there was an industrial kitchen with a pass-through window. They all had a plastic tray in hand and were making their way toward the window, placing their tray on the silver ledge once they got there. Each guest was served a plate of hot food after selecting from various choices. The main dish appeared to be a hot stew with salad. Then one by one, the executives went to a side table, grabbed a napkin wrapped around utensils as well as any condiments they wanted and sat at one of the wooden picnic tables within the building.

Nick approached the line and stood behind Amber. "How's it going?"

"Okay, I guess," Amber whispered. "They used the bathrooms and now we'll try a meal. I don't think they're in love with the whole concept yet. At this point, I already feel like I just want to get through it and on to next weekend."

"Yeah, well your boss thinks these retreats are going to be a huge success. He plans to do several a year and my guess is that you'll get to be the hostess."

Amber turned back to look at Nick with a frown. "I don't think I'm cut out for this. Maybe a business meeting or two. I could be a guest lecturer but a camp babysitter for a bunch of executives forced to live in the woods for a week, that's not me."

"It's not your boss either by the way he was dressed this morning. Those clothes look great on a fancy camp wear magazine, but I don't think it's quite what he needs here. If he stayed, he might have gotten them dirty, and we have no fancy laundromat in the park."

Amber giggled at Nick's sarcasm. "That's probably a great assessment. Joe doesn't like to get his hands dirty or wet."

"Don't take this the wrong way, but I don't like the guy. Something about him irritates me."

Amber stayed silent for a moment. "I think I know what you mean. He's the CEO of a prestigious company, attractive, rich, successful, but after being with him a bit, you feel sick to your stomach."

"Bingo, you forgot arrogant," Nick said as they approached the window. "Talk about being sick to your stomach, let's hope this food tastes good."

Amber laughed and turned toward her tray. She accepted the stew and salad and waited for Nick to load his tray. "By the way, how are you feeling?" They made their way over to the condiment section.

Nick shrugged as he pulled plastic utensils and small butter packets. "My right foot is still kind of numb, so we'll see what happens."

"I'm sure these bunks are not going to be the most comfortable. I hope that isn't a problem for you."

"I suppose it might be, but I don't plan on doing a lot of sleeping during the night. Better if I sit up and read a bit. I can nap while you're at all those interesting lectures."

Amber punched him in the arm. "Thanks for your support."

Nick laughed as the pair joined the other guests at the tables. The group was spread out over the first two picnic tables in the room. They ate quietly while Amber tried to loosen them up with generic questions. Nothing worked until Bob Flowers asked a question.

"Do you ever sneak real food in here?" The others giggled as they ate their stew.

"It doesn't taste that bad," Felix said. "I've had worse."

"No, I mean real food," Bob said. "Maybe pizza and something with a kick to wash it down. You know what I mean?"

"Oh," Felix said. "I got you."

The group laughed as they relaxed.

"I feel like I'm back at camp," Veronica said as she shook her head. "We used to think of some mean things to torture the goody two-shoes."

"Let's not have any torture, please," Amber said, nervously looking around.

"What fun activities do you have lined up for tonight?" Dante Valentino smiled as he watched Amber turn to him.

"It's a free day here at the camp. There are plenty of things you can choose to do and it's a beautiful fall day. They have hiking trails to the beach if you want to see the ocean. I left the trail maps on the corner table by the door. In addition to the trails, they have other things like horseshoes or archery or a games area. Later this evening, we'll have a bonfire."

"All that?" Dante asked with a smile.

"Unless you'd like to sit outside and read?" Amber offered in a quiet voice.

"There are other things I can think of to do outside," Dante said with a small leer in Amber's direction.

Veronica tossed her head. "Do we get to sing around the campfire and toast marshmallows?"

"If you'd like."

"What I'd like to do is listen to the latest tech podcast," Nancy Rogan replied with a frown.

Amber tried to look sympathetic. "It must be frustrating not to have access to Wi-Fi while you're here, but that is precisely why they are holding the retreat in the state park, so that everyone will be off the grid." She turned to the rest of the group. "We're so addicted to our phones and devices that it's hard to put them down."

"They happen to be the main focus of my job as CIO," Nancy spat.

"I realize," Amber said, trying to be diplomatic. "But our training this week will be through personal conversation."

Heads turned as they heard a loud snort from the other table, but it wasn't obvious who had made the noise.

Nick spoke up. "Why don't we give it a couple of days to see what happens. You never know, you may be very surprised at how much you enjoy this week."

The group grumbled and nodded as they went back to their meal. Amber looked at Nick and silently gave thanks.

17

M egan opened the front door when she heard the doorbell and Georgie flew into the foyer. "Sorry I'm late, but I had an errand."

"No worries," Megan said as she closed the door.

Dudley, Bella, and Smokey skidded along the foyer floor to see who was visiting. Once they reached Georgie, they performed a complete sniffing ritual to check out their new guest. Although it was October, Georgie always seemed to smell like the suntan lotion she wore daily to the beach. She scratched the dogs behind the ears and sent them on their way. "I'm here to see your mama. We've got work to do."

Turning to Megan, she asked, "Where do we go?"

"We're in the kitchen today. Marie put out something to snack on and rich, strong coffee."

"Sounds great," Georgie said as they made their way into the kitchen.

"I'm sure it will be," Megan said as she pulled out a chair for Georgie. Marie had set the table with delicate utensils and small China dishes. A charcuterie board was centered on the table.

"Wow," Georgie said as she looked at the table.

"We also talked about ordering a pizza but I think this may be enough and Marie made fresh cinnamon scones for dessert but why don't we start with coffee?" Megan poured for all three of them and added a splash of cream.

"These were Grandma Rose's favorite dishes," Megan said as she looked at the pattern of delicate flowers on the plate.

"They're beautiful and so delicate," Georgie agreed as she admired them.

"I think they're part of a set of Royal Copenhagen dinnerware. My great grandfather, John Stanford, brought them back from Europe as a gift for my great grandmother, Mary. According to my grandmother, he surprised Mary after one of his transatlantic voyages and she loved using them for company."

"Gorgeous."

"My grandmother, Rose, came to live in Misty Manor when she married my grandfather George, and she always loved these dishes as well. Mary was happy to have someone who cherished them with her."

"And now they're all yours," Georgie said as she reached across and squeezed her friend's hand.

"They are gorgeous," Marie said as she moved the charcuterie closer to Georgie. "Better that we use them. It would be a shame if they stayed in a cabinet collecting dust."

"I agree," Georgie said as she chose various meats and cheeses from the board.

Once they selected their food and had drinks in place, Megan approached the task at hand.

"I reached out to Pastor Lee. I haven't met him yet, but he's been managing the food pantry and the shelter for several years. He said he had the honor of meeting Rose and together they had a plan for the next several years. There's not an independent board for the shelter but I'm sure the main board for the Stanford Foundation has something in their minutes to acknowledge that. I'll have to ask Teddy."

Georgie took a sip of coffee. "I can tell you the food pantry and the shelter have been very well used during the summers."

"Why is that?" Marie asked. "I'm very excited to help with this cause but I'd like to understand more about its mission."

Megan leaned over to sample a few more items from the charcuterie board. "Georgie, correct me if I'm wrong, but Pastor Lee seemed to say there is an increased need in the summer. I would have thought it would be the winter months as a lot of the beach business is shut down. I know there are a lot of year-round families here now."

"It's all true, for different reasons," Georgie said. "The beach attracts a lot of teens during the summer as well as adults who tend not to go home or have a solid home to go to. The town is good about not allowing anyone to sleep on the beach all night or under the boardwalk for that matter. It was happening in the past and we had all sorts of problems with certain hygienic issues as well as garbage and other items being left on the beach. It wasn't safe for anyone.

"Rose was great about helping to establish a safe shelter for homeless people to sleep at night. It's managed by Pastor Lee and a group of volunteers. Two meals a day are provided to the guests." Georgie looked at Megan. "The beach is cleaned and swept daily with the tractor rake. Garbage, plastic, and other items are disposed of properly. Since Pastor Lee started the shelter, the beach stays beautiful and clean for all visitors. In addition, those that need help have a safe place to stay."

"That makes a lot of sense," Megan said. "Pastor Lee mentioned that the hospital regularly sends social workers and a nurse to the shelter to check if anything is needed."

"As far as I know," Georgie said. "By the end of the summer, I've usually identified the kids who are living at the shore without a proper home. Some are troubled. The social workers try to help, find them a job, and make sure they're healthy until they get back on their feet with school or their families. Pastor Lee runs a tight ship but does a really great job. No one is allowed to take up permanent residence. They're strict about activities, helping, and lights out. No alcohol or drugs are allowed. The Misty Point Police Department makes it a habit to check there as well."

Georgie looked at the others at the table. "Remember when that apartment building on the South end burned down? They used the shelter to help house the people who were displaced for a couple of weeks. Better than the school gymnasium."

"Yes, I definitely remember the fire," Marie said as she turned to Megan. "It was before you returned, so you wouldn't remember but your grandmother fed, housed, and clothed that group for a while. I don't think the foundation had approved the shelter as a charity at that point, but it was a priority from that moment on for your grandmother."

Megan thoughtfully nodded. "The shelter sounds like a great cause. Now I see the bigger picture. Marie, to answer your question, it seems that the food pantry is used to supply food to year-round families who need help but also to make food that is offered daily to those staying in the shelter."

"Who organizes the menu and does the cooking?" Marie asked while looking at both women.

They shook their heads. "I don't know, Marie," Megan replied. "But we have an appointment at the shelter tomorrow. That will be one of the many questions for Pastor Lee as we learn how it all works."

"I'd really love to help with the shelter. I've known of its existence, but not how it operates," Marie said, a bit of excitement in her voice.

Megan reached out and covered Marie's hand with her own. "Believe me, I knew you'd be perfect and I'm sure Pastor Lee would welcome any help he can get. It's all settled then. We have some great ideas to bring to our meeting tomorrow morning."

"Great," Georgie said with a lopsided grin as she looked at Megan. "That means you can now open the wine you promised me tonight."

Laughing, Megan got up and walked toward the counter when they heard the doorbell ring.

"I wonder who that is. Are you expecting anyone?" Marie asked with a frown.

"Not that I'm aware of. I'll check it out while you two work on the wine." Megan handed off the bottle as she walked out the door.

"Don't take too long or it may all be gone when you get back," Georgie said with a wink.

Megan shook her head and walked out into the foyer. She saw a shadow through the glass. She opened the door and jumped back when a bouquet of flowers was placed in front of her. She looked up in surprise. "Jonathan?"

18

As the light of day crept away, Amber and Nick sat outside the cabin and waited for their guests to return. After lunch, the group scattered to their luggage and the bathrooms. Once changed, they all disappeared, and Amber couldn't keep track of who was going where with whom. They had been warned to be back by 6:30 p.m. so they could have dinner and relax afterward.

Dante Valentino and Veronica Lane had returned an hour ago. Vernonia had picked up a book and began to read in the common area. Amber wasn't sure but she had a good idea it was the latest novel by a best-selling author. She giggled to herself. *What did she expect an executive to read?* It didn't always have to be industry magazines.

Dante immediately went to his bunk and took a nap. They were waiting for the other four guests to return.

"What time should we start the bonfire?" Amber asked as she looked at Nick.

He glanced at his watch. "By the time they get back here and eat, then change or shower, it will be close to 9:00pm."

Amber nodded and offered a small grin. "This feels like it was the longest day ever and we're not through yet."

Nick laughed. "I hear you. I'm not used to being out all day. My foot's numb and I have a headache. I hope I don't fall asleep in front of the fire tonight."

"Even if you do, Phil is here to tend to it, so you don't have to worry about that. He seems like a nice guy."

"Good, I'm glad. I don't remember Captain Davis saying anything about tending to campfires as part of security detail anyway."

"I wouldn't want you to get burned. Megan would have my head."

Nick laughed as he picked up a stick and started scratching at the dirt. "I imagine she would be upset, but remember, what happens here stays here. You're not to tell tales about my fatigue, numb foot, or anything else."

Amber pointed to herself with mock surprise. "Who me?"

"I'm dead serious. She's upset as it is that I'm here. Let's not give her any reason to complain about me going back to the force."

"Nick, what you tell Megan is your business. I'm hoping I survive the week and have a job by the time it's all over. This whole thing fills me with dread. I know it's the inaugural stay, but the routine is feeling very awkward."

"Let's think positive. The week will probably fly by. One day at a time, one hour at a time if we need to. It's a NJ State Park. Tonight, we have free time. Tomorrow all the lectures and trust exercises start. Maybe one of them will fail to catch the other when they fall backward. Other than that, what's the worst thing that could possibly happen?"

19

"Jonathan, what are you doing here?"

"Hi, Megan. It's great to see you," Jonathan said as he placed the large bouquet in her hands and stepped forward into the foyer. She noticed his expensive cologne as he paused to gather her in his arms. Marie and Georgie peeked out of the kitchen with widened eyes.

Jonathan was the son of Theodore Harrison Carter. Theodore or Teddy as they referred to him had been the estate attorney for many years as well as a very close friend to her grandmother Rose. When Megan was young, she and Jonathan had a play date or two, but then Jonathan went to England with his mother and stayed there with family when she died of cancer. He recently returned to America to reconnect with his father. Teddy had taken the opportunity to reintroduce him to Megan, hoping his son could take his place when he retired. He thought it would be poetic to have the next generation of each family continue to chair the Stanford Foundation and charities set up by Rose. Teddy also wanted them to continue to cherish the beautiful Grand Victorian Mansion, Misty Manor, as well as the rest of the property encompassing most of Misty Point, NJ. All the better if the families happen to marry.

"Jonathan, I'm surprised to see you," Megan stuttered as Jonathan leaned forward to kiss her cheek. "I thought you went back to England."

"I've returned to the Jersey Shore. I had to finish some business in London. After that, I rented out my flat and now I'm back."

"Really?"

"Yes, and I couldn't wait to see you." Jonathan looked up to see Marie and Georgie. "Oh, I didn't realize you had company. I'm interrupting, aren't I?"

"We were just having a small meeting," Megan stammered as she tried to regain her composure. "About one of the charities as a matter of fact."

"That's great. I don't want to get in the way, but that gives me a great reason to take you to dinner tomorrow night. There's probably so much I need to catch up on."

"Well, yes a lot has happened."

"Great, how about I pick you up at 7:00 p.m. tomorrow then? I heard there's a great new restaurant in town." Jonathan leaned forward and bussed Megan's cheek again before he waved to Marie and Georgie, turned, and headed out the door.

The foyer remained in total silence except for Dudley pawing at Megan's leg.

"You'd better come back to the kitchen for that glass of wine," Marie said as Megan turned away from the door.

"That was a bit of a shock." Georgie pushed a chilled glass of White Merlot into Megan's hand as Marie took the flowers to place them in a vase.

"I thought he was going to stay in London," Marie said.

"So did I and Teddy never mentioned he was coming back to the States."

"You're going to dinner tomorrow night?" Georgie asked with a grin.

"I really didn't get a chance to respond."

"You can always call and cancel."

Megan picked up her wine and took a long sip. "I don't know. Let me call Teddy and see what's happening. If Jonathan is replacing him, then he does need to be brought up to date on a few things. If I need to have dinner with him, then this week would be best while Nick is away."

"Be careful, Megan. I think Jonathan has completely different ideas than simply being an estate attorney." Marie sniffed as she refilled the glasses. "When Teddy retires, you're free to choose whomever you want to counsel you. We don't even know if Jonathan's a good attorney. His experience in Europe may not translate well to America."

"Let's take a step back and a deep breath. Thank you both for your concern. I need to call Teddy and do a bit of thinking, but that will be later. In the meantime, let's have our wine and relax."

20

Amber watched as three more of the executive guests wandered back to the cabin. "That's five of them. We're still waiting for Felix Cooper."

Nick looked up. He was sitting in an Adirondack chair rubbing his right thigh. "These chairs aren't exactly comfortable for someone with a numb leg. So where is everyone right now?"

"Most are in the cabin. I think Nancy Rogan may have gone to take a shower, and I'm sure they're all hungry." Amber looked at her watch. "I don't think we can wait much longer to take them to the mess hall. Felix will have to eat when he gets back. I can bring a tray back to the cabin, but it will be cold."

"Cold food is better than none," Nick said with a shrug. "Did you happen to notice when he left? Was he dressed in a bathing suit or running clothes?"

"I have no idea," Amber said. "Why?"

"I could go look for him in case he got hurt. The beaches in the park don't have any lifeguards. The park is big, but not that large that he couldn't find some way to get back."

Amber shook her head. "I have no idea."

"Why don't we gather the other guests and bring them to dinner.

Let's ask them if anyone saw Felix leave. If we have a general direction, I can take a walk to see if I can find him."

"Do you want help?"

"No, you concentrate on the guests. Let Phil feed everyone and start the fire when it's time."

"Sounds good. Phil has everything ready. He stacked the wood next to the pit earlier today and we have water and an extinguisher if necessary."

"It's a plan then. Let's go get the rest of the troops."

Amber and Nick walked into the cabin and located their five guests. Several were in their bunk. Bob Flowers was staring at the ceiling with a frown on his face. Veronica was now reading a fashion magazine. Dante was listening to music on his phone. Nick assumed he had music downloaded as the Wi-Fi was not active in the cabin. Nancy and Alberto sat in chairs in front of a cold hearth starting off into space. The group appeared quiet, but all looked up when Amber and Nick arrived.

"Anyone hungry? Why don't we go over to the mess hall and see what lovely surprise we have for dinner?" Amber tried to sound cheerful. "By the way, has anyone seen or heard from Felix? I wouldn't want him to miss the delicious food."

"He probably saw the menu for tonight and ran onto the Parkway to save himself," Bob Flowers said sarcastically. The group laughed at Bob's remark as they got ready to leave but no one had any information about Felix.

Nick whispered in Amber's ear. "You take them to dinner. I'll do a little search of Felix's bunk to see if there's a note or anything that can guide us."

Once the group had filed out of the cabin, Nick went over to the bunk Felix had chosen. Out of habit, he checked his pockets for gloves and chided himself when he didn't find any. He pulled the blankets down and slid his hand under the pillow to see if anything was stored there. Finding nothing, he looked at the area around the bunk and once again found nothing except casual wear. Stepping back, he spied a knapsack stowed underneath the bunk. With a grunt due to some back pain, he bent over and pulled it out. He opened it and quickly flipped through Felix's belongings. He found a wallet, a phone, some headphones, a book about bird watching, and money. At the bottom, he found clean underwear and socks. There was also another pair of sneakers underneath the bunk. Nick took a minute to check the shoes but didn't find anything hidden or strange tucked inside.

He wasn't expecting to find directions to where Felix had gone, but perhaps he'd know what direction in which he started. If he didn't show up soon, Nick would have to make some calls about putting together a small search party. *What were the chances he left his stuff and simply disappeared so he wouldn't have to attend the retreat?* Nick initially thought the chances were high, but he didn't think Felix would have left his wallet or phone if that were the case. He needed to start his own search and call his Captain to inform him what was happening since they made the arrangement with Portal Health. Then he'd inform the NJ State Park Police. There would be grief tomorrow if Felix didn't show up.

Nick put everything back together, grabbed a jacket and left the cabin to find Amber. He walked into the mess hall. Amber and her guests were gathered at the two wooden tables located next to each other. The meal tonight was roasted chicken with red potatoes and some unidentified green vegetable. Decent fare for camping in a state park. They had coffee, soda, water and alcohol-free beer and wine. Not a popular choice for this crowd.

Waving toward Amber he nodded toward the door when she looked up. She politely excused herself and made her way to him. "What's up? Any news?"

"Nothing," Nick said shaking his head. "His wallet, money, phone, and bird watching book are safely tucked in his bunk. I don't get the impression he snuck out to buy liquor or visit the closest bar, especially if he was on foot. I checked the parking lot earlier and there was one car. I saw a couple hiking through the park, so I'm assuming it belonged to them and they were random visitors although I can't be sure of anything."

"Okay," Amber said with a tremor. "What's our next step?"

"I'll go for a little hike toward the bird observatory. If necessary, I'll try the beach as well and see if I can find him. They're the most common trails. If he doesn't show up, I'll have to call the station and let the Captain know. You'll have to give me the key to the office when I get back so I can use the landline."

"Fine. Just let me know what you need me to do."

"Keep everyone together. Have Phil help you with the fire and do your thing. I can't text you, but I'll get a message to you."

"Okay, be safe. I don't want to worry about you, and I don't want to be the one to tell Megan something happened. I'll fill a tray and bring it back to the cabin for you when you get back."

"I'll be fine," Nick said as he waved her away. He started walking toward the parking lot but stopped at the cabin to retrieve a large tactical LED flashlight torch from his bag. Truth be told he was a bit nervous about having a problem if his leg throbbed or went completely numb. He was getting stronger, but he hadn't regained his confidence and Nick realized the only way he could regain his verve was to start getting out in the world again.

Nick approached the parking lot and stopped at the brown wooden plastic enclosed sign highlighting a map of walking trails around the state park. He only had twenty minutes before it would be pitch black. He had no idea which direction Felix may have gone or whether he was still in the state park. Nick sighed and studied the map again. He decided he would start with the green trail. There was a lot of bird sighting on that trail according to the description and given that he had found the bird book, Nick could only guess Felix would choose that direction before seeing the beach.

Nick started off toward the green trail. He followed a trodden path and looked for reflective green post signs at regular intervals. The only problem was the signs only glowed when they reflected a source of light. Nick couldn't shine a light on them if he didn't know where they were to begin with, and he didn't want to risk taking the light off the path when it became pitch dark. Things would be that much worse if he fell and couldn't get back to the cabin. Following the path, he turned once or twice when he thought he heard someone or something in the brush behind him. Although the noise wasn't close by, he called out in hopes that Felix could answer especially if he was lying hurt somewhere. He continued to call his name as he walked back toward the direction, he thought the noise had come from. He heard a similar noise once or twice but couldn't pin the location down.

The sun had set, and it was almost completely dark. Nick heard small scampering noises as he walked the path and was sure there were many small animals and birds that were disturbed by his presence. He continued to call out every twenty feet and then stopped to listen. Quiet surrounded him in the woods. The light of a half-moon broke through the clouds and the temperature dropped as time went by.

Nick hit his watch and checked the time in the luminescent glow. He had been gone an hour and had no new information to show for it. He was hoping Felix somehow had returned to the cabin with a long story about being lost. Nick would be annoyed but wouldn't care if Felix had snuck out of the campground and returned. Nick only needed to make sure the guy was accounted for.

He turned and headed back to camp. He took a minute to shine his flashlight until he saw a green post marker confirming he was heading in the right direction. Ten steps later he heard the strange noise again off to his left in the scrub. He stopped and swept the flashlight on the ground in-between the trees. He thought he heard something in the brush about ten feet off the path. Holding the light high, he started to make his way off the path. Nick bent to pick up a large branch to sweep the brush to make sure there was nothing underneath, but he froze when he felt something cold against the back of his neck. He then heard a click and voice whisper in his ear, "Don't move."

21

Megan opened the front door to let the dogs outside. They immediately ran toward the beach scrub as she wandered onto the front porch with her wineglass in hand. Georgie had left a couple of hours ago and Marie had settled in her room after cleaning the kitchen.

Jonathan was a nice guy and Megan felt a small connection with him. She didn't really believe he was angling to be with her just to get his hands on her fortune. But then, you never know these days. She was a very rich multimillionaire. At any rate, she was committed to Nick. She wondered how he was doing his first day on assignment. Although the cabin was reasonably accommodated, it couldn't be as comfortable as his room in Misty Manor. Megan hoped he was doing well.

As far as Jonathan was concerned, she had some thinking to do. Megan had been able to learn more about the foundation and now she felt she was ready to discuss a complete list of all the charities involved with the Stanford Foundation. She also wanted a complete overview of the annual grants and reports that were filed. Megan wanted to keep Grandmother Rose's charities and reputation alive and enhance things where she could. Needs were always changing as well as the support the foundation could offer. She had taken enough time to grieve. She needed time to adjust to her changed life's circumstances and to learn all she could about Misty Point. It was time for her to start managing her own version of the foundation and future. Whether Jonathan would be part of it, she had no idea, but she would start with calling Teddy in the morning.

22

Nick didn't move while trying to assess his situation. He was out in the woods, in the dark. Numb leg, back pain. *What the hell was he thinking coming back to work?* He wasn't going to be able to move fast enough to avoid contact with a bullet. Even if he blinded the guy with his flashlight, he wouldn't get far. He didn't want to die in the woods. "Easy there. I'm a cop. What do you want?"

"Nothing," came the answer with a laugh as the gun was holstered and put away. "I want to keep you sharp. You're training to return to duty."

Nick stood up straight and turned around. "Luther? You're an ass," he yelled. "What the hell was that?" He was practically shouting and hoped Luther didn't see how hard he was shaking.

"Hey, I'm sorry buddy. I see someone crawling around in the dark in the scrub. First, I wasn't sure it was you, but then I was waiting to see if you remembered your training? I could have taken you out before you even knew I was here."

Nick was furious and glad Luther couldn't see his face, but he knew he was right. "I think you're forgetting I wasn't a black-ops operative like you."

"No, but we know you had a lot more training than basic police duty. Time to remember your roots pal."

Nick took a breath. "What the hell are you doing here anyway?"

"Looking out for you." Luther lightly punched Nick's arm in the dark.

"Yeah, I get it, but like I said, what the hell are you doing here?"

"Like I said, keeping an eye on you. You and Megan are funny because I promised her, I'd keep an eye on you while you have me keeping an eye on her. You two seriously need to get your stuff together. Anyway, I told her I'd take my run out here in the park tonight and give you a quick check in."

Nick took a deep breath, relaxed, and shook his head. "Just so happens, I'm glad you're here. We have six executives, none of which are happy. They were all forced to come to the program. They had free time this afternoon to relax and get equilibrated. Problem is, only five of them came back to the cabin. I'm out here searching for number six."

"Are you sure he didn't just take off?" Luther asked as he looked around him. The breeze blew by both men, the rustling leaves sounding more ominous as it did.

"I have no idea where the guy is. I searched his bunk, and all his stuff is there including wallet, phone, and a bird book."

"Well, he's not looking at any birds this time of night."

"Exactly, so either he's hurt or took off. I'm going to have to call it in to the Captain and the State Park Police, but since you've been running around here, I'll assume you haven't seen anything out of the ordinary."

"Nothing." Luther shook his head. "But it's a big place. I'm only doing a light ten miles or so."

"The guy couldn't have gotten far if he was walking. I figure he must be close if he's still in the park. I heard some noises in the brush, but now I'm wondering if that was you."

"Believe me bro, if I was hiding out, you would not have heard me. So, it was either an animal or he could be hurt. We're not going to find anything tonight. I don't think anyone is here. All I feel is stillness right now. I used to be able to smell them - people, soldiers. Let's walk a bit and call out. If we don't get an answer, you better call the station and report. I'll come back by daybreak with some of the guys and do extra reconnaissance in the area."

"You can take the soldier out of the war, but not the war out of the soldier," Nick mused. "But I'd appreciate any extra eyes you can lend me."

"Sure, we'll bring a couple of sat phones so we can stay in touch."

"I should have brought one with me, but no one expected this assignment to amount to anything."

"If I was doing an assignment in this park, I'd always have a satellite phone. It's the only way to get a quick line if you need one here."

"Agreed brother. Let's do some walking and talking. See if we can find anyone," Nick said as he walked out of the brush and started down the dark trail with Luther.

Nick and Luther walked as much of the trail as they could using the tactical flashlight and calling out Felix's name. They heard animals in the brush and movement among the trees but heard no response to their calls. After an hour, they retraced their steps and headed toward camp. When they pulled close, the fire pit was blazing, and lights were in sight. Luther stopped and pulled off the trail.

"I'm going to fade off right here, brother. No sense having to explain who I am to the crowd."

Nick nodded. "Okay, I'll go check the camp to see if the guy returned. If not, I'll call Captain Davis and let him know our status. Maybe he can call the State Park Police. Amber will have to call her boss as well."

"Sounds like a plan," Luther said. "As soon as you wake up, check the front porch. There'll be a package with your name on it. I'll have a fully charged sat phone in there. If this guy is back, just let us know. If not, we'll be in touch."

"Appreciate all your help," Nick said as he clapped Luther on the shoulder and turned toward the camp.

23

Nick walked towards the firepit. From a distance he could see the high flames dancing and smell the fragrance of burning wood. Normally, he found the smell relaxing and comforting but not tonight.

He couldn't see facial features in the dark but started counting the silhouettes of people sitting in chairs in front of the fire. He found seven in all. He cheered hoping that Felix had returned after simply getting lost in the wood, but when he rounded the chairs, he saw Amber sitting next to her boss and five of the executives. Joe Daman was giving a pep talk to the other executives who appeared to be rolling their eyes and concentrating more on toasting marshmallows than the concept of leadership and branding.

Nick caught Amber's eye and nodded off to the side. She jumped out of her chair and met him in the dark, fifty feet behind the others. "Did you find him?"

Nick shook his head. "No, I walked the trail for quite a while. As a matter of fact, Luther showed up and walked with me."

"Luther? How did he get involved?" Amber crossed her arms as she waited.

"Megan asked him to keep an eye on us, which is insulting except it turns out I needed his help. Don't mention him to anyone at any time though." Nodding toward the fire Nick asked, "What's Daman doing here?"

"Funny you should ask. I was thinking I should let him know about Felix if we turned up empty tonight, but then he suddenly pops in to see how we're all doing. I had no idea he was planning to return tonight."

"Did you tell him?"

"Yes, I explained that Felix went off for the free period but never returned."

"What was his reaction?"

"He was quiet. He didn't get angry. I was afraid he would when I told him we lost one of the guests."

"Did he question you?"

"No, not really. He hasn't said much at all. He seems to be trying very hard to make light conversation around the fire to distract the others."

"I find that interesting," Nick said more to himself than Amber. "I need to get into the park office. Do you have the key? I have to call the station and put Captain Davis on alert that we have someone missing. He made me agree to tell him anything that's going on. They can put a BOLO out on the streets in case Felix shows up at a hospital and they can call the NJ State Park Police since they would have jurisdiction to do the investigation and search. Overall, I'm getting a bad feeling about this whole event."

"What a nightmare," Amber said, shaking her head.

"What's going on back here?"

Nick and Amber whirled around to find Joe Daman standing right behind them.

"Hey, don't sneak up on us like that. You scared me," Amber said lightly as she chided her boss.

"Sorry, I didn't mean to do that. Just wondering if we've made any progress with our little problem."

Nick shook his head. "So far, nothing. I did all the searching I could before nightfall. After dark, I walked the trail calling out but no response. I'm going to inform the local police and the NJ State Park Police. If necessary, we'll start organizing search parties tomorrow."

Daman shook his head as he visibly became agitated. "How many people usually disappear in a state park? The guy probably took off. He'll call his boss and tell him to screw off for making him come to a program like this."

Nick paused before he spoke. "The answer to your first question is it depends on the state park. You may be right, and his boss will be one of the first phone calls that's made to see if anyone has heard from the guy."

"This is unbelievable," Daman said, shaking his head. "A few people in a cabin and you can't even keep track of them."

Amber blew out a breath, reached up and raked her fingers through her hair. "I'm sorry. It's not like I could accompany them all on the break."

"I didn't mean you, Amber. I was talking to our security."

Nick crossed his arms and let out a laugh. "I'm sorry, I didn't realize your guests were under house arrest. I also don't remember receiving any specific security protocols from you or your company regarding free time."

"You can bet that will be remediated in the future, if there is a future."

Nick stood fully upright, staring at Daman in silence for a full minute before he turned to Amber. "Please get the key for the office so I can make a few phone calls. I need the station to put out that BOLO in case something happened outside the park."

"Of course, I'll be right back." Amber turned and ran off toward the cabin. As she did, Bob Flowers called out after her.

"Hey, is it a crime to play some music around here? Anything to liven it up a bit."

Nick turned to Daman. "Do you have an emergency listing on file for these executives?"

"I'm sure they had to fill something out with an emergency contact, but I don't have the paperwork."

"Then I'd suggest you contact your company and get that information. After that, you'd better go back to your guests and try to calm them down," Nick suggested as he pointed toward the large bonfire. "Maybe perform a few magic tricks to keep them entertained."

Daman shot Nick a nasty look before turning to the firepit.

A few minutes later, Amber returned with the key in hand. "Here you go," she said as she handed him a large wooden stick with a key attached.

"Thanks," Nick said as he immediately removed the key and handed the large stick back to her. "I'll be holding on to this key for now. I'm going to the office. I don't know how long I'll be but when the kindergarten tires out, get them back into the cabin. No one leaves except that idiot boss of yours. I'll let you know if I hear anything when I get back."

"Okay, be safe," Amber said with a worried look on her face.

"You take care of yourself," Nick said as he gave her a quick hug about her shoulders. "I'm not comfortable with what's going on at the moment."

24

———————

Nick opened the door of the office and walked inside. He found the light switch and flipped it on. Walking around the heavily varnished wooden desk, he found the desk phone on top of an old-fashioned blotter with pens, pencils, and paper at the ready. It took him a few tries, but he was finally able to dial an outside line. Captain Davis picked up on the fourth ring and he wasn't in a good mood.

"Davis."

"Hey, it's Nick Taylor, calling from North Marsh State Park."

"I was trying to figure out who the hell was calling me on a Sunday night at 10:00 p.m. but I guess we solved that now."

"Sorry about that, but this couldn't wait."

"What's going on over there? Someone burn a marshmallow?" Davis laughed at his own sarcastic attempt at humor.

"I wish," Nick said. "One of the guests has gone missing."

"What do you mean gone missing?" Davis's raised voice matched his irritation.

"He went out on free time and never returned."

"He probably took off. The whole event sounds hokey to me."

"It's possible, but I'm following protocol. I'm calling you and the

State Park Police and if he isn't back tomorrow, we'll have to start a search party."

"If he didn't leave, he's probably off to no good somewhere."

"I agree but wanted you to have a heads up. Who's on the desk?"

"Peters should be on," Davis said. "And if he's not, better call me back and let me know."

"Will do. I'll have Peters put out a BOLO for the hospitals and find out what kind of car Felix drives in case he had it stashed close by. But if the guy wanted to leave, I don't think he would have left his wallet and phone behind. He's a bird watcher so he's probably the only guest who looked forward to being here for a week with pay."

"I don't know how in the hell you get involved in these things, Taylor. Your girlfriend isn't there, is she?"

Nick barked, "No, she has absolutely nothing to do with this whole adventure."

"Good and keep it that way. I don't have to point out to you to tread lightly here. The State Park Police have jurisdiction with these types of things. Other than being asked to provide a suggestion for private security, the local police are not involved. Make sure you call me in the morning to give me an update anyway."

"You got it," Nick said as he heard a click. Without hesitation, he disconnected the phone and then called the station. Officer Peters picked up and Nick quickly relayed the situation. He worked with Peters until the BOLO went out. All the local hospitals and clinics would receive an alert matching the description of Felix Cooper in case they had an unidentified patient come in. Next, they conferenced the State Park Police and put them on notice that someone was missing. They arranged to have someone arrive in the park within minutes to take a report and get more information. The State Park Police had an amazing search and rescue team, complete with dogs, but Nick wasn't sure what timeline they used to call them out.

Peters pulled Nick's attention back when he stated he would have another officer start making calls to Salacia Medical Supply to see if there had been any contact or if they had another number to reach him. Without much else to do until daylight, Nick disconnected the call. He looked at the phone for a few seconds and then hurriedly dialed another number. It rang six or seven times before someone picked up.

"Hello?"

"Megan? It's me, Nick." Nick shifted at hearing her voice and sat in the desk chair.

"Nick, I almost didn't answer. I didn't recognize the number."

"I know, this is the landline in the state park main office."

"How are you holding up? Is everything okay?"

"Not really. Where are you? Are you alone?"

Megan was on alert as she looked out toward the ocean. The dogs were still running near the water's edge stopping to sniff and jump at various finds along the way. "Yes, I'm on the front porch watching the dogs. What's wrong? Should I call them in?"

"No, everything is fine there, as far as I know, but we're having a little issue here at the park."

"Do you need me to come over? Do you need anything?"

"No, we're okay for now." Nick spent the next 15 minutes telling Megan about the missing executive and the plan for a search if Felix didn't show up tomorrow.

"Do you need volunteers? We can help find people on this end. I'm sure there are a lot of people I can get to volunteer."

"No, don't do anything yet. Let's wait until tomorrow and we'll let the State Park Police do their investigation first."

"Okay, but I'm only a call away." Megan peered out at the full moon illuminating the beach. Dudley and Bella still romped on the sand and Megan noticed her wine glass was empty. "I hope you get some rest tonight. I miss you."

"I miss you too." Nick was quiet for a few seconds. "As much as this has already turned into a circus, we both know I need to do this to move on."

"I know," Megan said, surprised she was choked up. The wine must be making her melancholy. "Please send me some sort of an update tomorrow and let me know what's happening. Sneak back to the office if you must."

"I will," Nick said in a soft voice. "Love you."

"Love you, too." Megan continued to hold the phone to her ear after she heard the call disconnect. She realized this was the first night since Nick's near-death experience that he was not with her in Misty Manor.

Nick placed the receiver down and stood up from the desk. He wanted to get back to the cabin to make sure everyone was accounted for before it was time for lights out. He could see the bonfire in the distance through the office window, but it was dwindling, and a few people may have just been waiting for it to die out. With nothing else to do in the office, Nick turned out the lights, relocked the door and made his way on the path toward the cabin.

One hundred yards from the cabin, Nick heard noises in the scrub. He stopped and looked around but didn't see anyone. He began to walk but stop when he heard someone moaning. Not sure of what was in the brush he walked another ten feet before pulling off the path and moving five feet into the scrub. He quietly skirted two or three trees before turning his tactical flashlight on and directing the beam toward the noise. All movement abruptly stopped as Nick looked into the faces of Veronica Lane and Dante Valentino. They were half dressed and entwined in an intimate position. "Really?"

"Hey, cut the damn light, will ya?" Dante yelled as he held his arm up to shield his eyes.

"Pardon me, I didn't realize you knew each other," Nick said as he turned off the flashlight. "As a matter of fact, I thought you both said you weren't acquainted with each other."

"That's none of your damn business," Veronica said angrily. "You're not our father so get lost."

Nick shook his head and walked toward the path. "You have ten minutes to get back to the cabin. I already have one person missing and the State Park Police as well as local police have been notified. They should be here within minutes."

Nick turned around and walked the rest of the way toward the cabin. Joe Daman was still in front of the bonfire, punching buttons on his cell phone without response. The fire was being tamped down by Phil Beckman. The rest of the executives were gone. Nick knew where Veronica and Dante were but not the other three, so he walked up toward the cabin.

Amber was in the front of the room, helping two of the guests, Nancy Rogan and Alberto Ortiz get ready to turn in. "What's happening, Nick?"

"The State Park Police are on their way to take a report. The Misty Point Police are already putting BOLO's out to the hospitals and clinics. Were you able to find emergency contact information for this guy?"

"Joe was trying to phone someone to see what they have on file."

"Judging by his behavior, and the fact that we have very little service, I'm going to guess he's not having any success. By the way, Veronica and Dante are playing house over in the woods."

"Are you kidding me?" Amber's face registered surprise.

"Not at all," Nick said as he shook his head. "Where's Bob Flowers?"

Amber searched the room. "He was here a few moments ago. Perhaps he went to the bathroom to get ready for the night."

"He'd better be back in ten minutes. This whole thing has been a circus so far. We don't need to make this worse."

"You got that right. I am so fired after all of this is over," Amber said with a grimace.

"I'm thinking you'll be better off. Megan's looking for help with the foundation. Let her hire you full time."

"I think she'd rather have you," Amber pointed out.

"I'm going back to the station, unless I get suspended as well."

They turned when they heard a noise and watched Bob Flowers make his way into the cabin. He was slightly off balance but had a smile on his face.

"Bob, are you okay?" Amber asked as she hurried to his side.

"Meee? I'm fine," Bob said as he waved his hand. Amber turned toward Nick.

"Bob, you look a bit unsteady. What's up?" Nick asked as he walked over and put a hand on his arm. As he did an empty bottle of

Jack Daniel's dropped to the floor. Nick bent over and picked it up. "Bob? You been sipping on this all day?"

"I had a little during dinner and around the fire. I snuck it into my cup." Bob started snickering and Nick had to wave the smell of alcohol away from his face before he became nauseous.

"I see," Nick said. "I'm glad there aren't any cars around here. Bet you can't really walk a straight line right now, can you?"

"Why the hell would I want to?" Bob said with a laugh which then ended abruptly in a burp. "Sorry about that."

"That's okay, Bob. Why don't I just walk you over to your bunk, so we know you get into the right one." Amber rolled her eyes at Nick.

"Say, that's a great idea," Bob said with a smile as he threw his arm around Amber's shoulders. "I think you may have to help me relax in bed, if you know what I mean." Bob exhaled an alcohol laden breath in her direction as he winked.

"I know what you mean," Amber drawled as she fought to keep nausea at bay. "I really want to make sure that you don't accidentally hit your head on the top bunk although I think your head's going to hurt quite a bit tomorrow either way."

"You're a peach." Bob slurred his words as he continued to stagger toward his bed.

Nick turned at a knock on the screen door to find two police officers standing outside.

"Amber." When she turned, he jabbed his thumb toward the door. "Come outside as soon as you can."

"You got it." She turned when she felt Bob pull on her waist.

"Do you want to get in first?"

"No, Bob. I like to be closer to the bathroom. Why don't you go first? Watch your head."

"Okay honey," he said as he half stumbled and slid into the bunk. Thankfully it was part of the wall, or it may have collapsed. He took a few tries to straighten out and place his head on the pillow.

"Now, you roll on your side and face the wall while I climb in. I'm bashful." Amber watched as he complied, satisfied that if he vomited, he wouldn't choke. As she suspected, he was unconscious in seconds.

"You handled that fairly well," Nancy said. "The man needs an intervention."

"I imagine that's why HR sent him to this program, but I'm sure they weren't aware that would happen. Sorry, I must go," Amber said as she then turned and went out to the porch to speak with Nick and the State Park Police.

25

Twenty minutes later, Nick and Amber returned to the cabin. They had spent time with the State Park Officers filing the report, offering as much information as they could. Joe Daman had joined them on the porch and added what little information he knew about the guests that had been registered for the retreat.

The small group exchanged phone numbers, for when anyone had service, and made a specific plan to communicate all information so all would be updated. If Felix was not back by morning, the park police would start with the search and rescue dogs who had a stellar reputation in the department. It was only hours until daybreak anyway.

Nick and Amber sat quietly in the back of the room after counting the executives to make sure all had returned. Bob Flowers was loudly snoring in his bunk. Veronica Lane and Dante Valentino were in their respective bunks. Alberto Ortiz and Nancy Rogan were sitting in chairs in the corner of the room, reading via flashlight. They had continued to attempt to connect to the internet, hoping there was less traffic at night, but to no avail. The signal was permanently blocked in the state park.

"What do you think happened to Felix? What is your gut

instinct?" Amber watched Nick's face as he tried to organize his thoughts.

"If it was Veronica, Dante, or Bob, I'd almost be sure they decided to take off. But I just don't get that impression with Felix. He didn't seem miserable or devious. Plus, if he was really going to leave, I'm sure he would have taken his phone and wallet."

"That's not good," Amber said.

"No, but we'll hopefully find out tomorrow. Alberto Ortiz and Nancy Rogan look like stiff personalities, but they don't look devious. I'm sure they're not happy to be here either but they seem prepared to suck it up for a week." Nick looked up at Amber. "I know there was a lot going on during lunch. I don't remember any specific comments from anyone about visiting a certain area. Did anyone ask you for directions or strange advice during or after lunch?"

Amber shook her head. "Not really. We ate lunch. They were excused and told to be back for dinner and the bonfire. Some changed clothing, some didn't, and they all took off."

"Did you happen to see if Felix wandered off with anyone in particular?"

Amber shook her head as she tried to visualize the moment.

"No. It seems to me they all just moved out en masse."

"I can't remember any specifics," Nick said. "It seems some were initially milling about, mostly complaining."

"Honestly, I was trying to finalize the agenda for tomorrow and set up the first talk. I wasn't paying attention to what they were doing. I didn't think I had to. I'm not babysitting." Amber ran her hands through her hair. "What I do remember is that Felix seemed strange when we were doing the introductions."

"True. Do one thing for me. When you relax, try to keep a log of everything you remember from today. Make sure you include any significant comments or questions. Do it while the information is fresh in your mind. We may never need it, but if we refer to it later, there may be a clue about something we don't realize is important right now."

"Okay, I doubt I'm going to sleep, so I'll do that tonight." Amber frowned as she continued to twirl her hair.

"Great, thank you," Nick said with a smile. "I'll do the same thing. I'm going to sit at the desk and read for a bit in case someone else wants to wander or if our friend returns during the night."

"Are you going to be able to stay up all night? Do you want me to split the night with you?"

"I'll be fine, Amber. Thanks for offering. I think you'd better get your sleep so you're ready to handle this group tomorrow. I'll catch a couple of hours nearer to daybreak."

"Are you sure, Nick? Megan is going to kill me if she knows you're up all night and not getting rest."

"I'm sure," Nick said, annoyed. "Go on, get ready to turn in and get some sleep while you can."

Amber looked at Nick for a few seconds. She held a small smile, but her eyes watered as if she was about to cry. "Thank you for being here. Thanks for being my friend. I don't know what I would have done if some other security guard was here."

Nick reached out and gave her a brotherly hug. After patting her on the back several times, he pulled back and urged her on her way. He then made his way to the desk, pulled out a lined pad with a pen and readied himself for a long night.

26

Nick stirred and opened his eyes. He lay on his back, listening to the sounds around him. His back reminded him he was in a bunk, in a cabin, in the state park. What he registered was the sound of birds. *How the hell many birds were out in the woods?* They were very loud this morning. He had read until 3:30 a.m. and then finally hit his bunk and fell asleep. There was no noise from within the dark cabin. He quietly sat up and started counting people. There were seven people in the cabin. Five executives, Amber, and himself.

Nick didn't think anyone else was awake, but if they were, they were still. Bob Flowers was snoring heavily, and Nick anticipated he would be in his bunk for a good part of the day.

Nick looked toward the windows. It was dark outside; however, he could see a lighter gray in the background. He stood up and made his way to the porch. True to his word, Luther had left a small box with Nick's name on it. Nick opened the box and found a satellite phone. He made sure it was on and active although he knew Luther would never have left anything he didn't personally check out. Holding the phone, he took the opportunity to walk around the outside of the cabin and then make his way toward the bathrooms. His gait was stiff because his leg didn't have time to warm up. He didn't see anything out of the ordinary, but it was still dark. Sunrise was twenty minutes away.

Amber wandered onto the porch when he returned. She pulled the sweater she was wearing tighter around her frame. "What's up? Did you hear anything?"

"No. I counted bodies in the cabin, and I think it's just the five executives and us. I was up until early morning but no word."

"I was praying I would wake up and find all six of them in the cabin with some stupid explanation."

They both turned as they saw a man in dark clothes walking up the path. They collectively held their breath as they waited for him to come closer and then realized it was the camp manager they hired. He saw them staring and waved.

"Howdy, good morning. Hope you slept well last night. Bit chilly this morning."

Amber raised her hand and waived back without speaking.

"I'm going into the mess hall and get some bacon and flapjacks going, but it's probably going to be another hour before the food is ready, so have the guests take their showers or whatever they want in the meantime."

"Of course, they're not up yet, so I think we have time," she replied in a whispered voice. She was hoping they slept as long as possible since the morning already looked like it would be hectic. She turned to Nick. "Where the hell did he sleep last night?"

"That's a good question. I'm going to find out, although I think there's a small bunk for staff in the back of the mess hall. I want to take a quick shower and change," Nick said. "The park police will be here soon and if we have no other information, we'll have to start searching."

Amber felt sick to her stomach. She blew out a big breath and said, "What do you want me to do in the meantime?"

"Exactly what he said. Have them clean up, but don't let anyone leave until we have a better handle on police activities this morning.

Bob isn't going anywhere for a while. I have a feeling Veronica and Dante will sleep late as well."

"Okay, I'll try to contain them," Amber said as she looked around the small camp.

"I have to call Megan and let her know what's going on. I don't want her to hear about it from the news or an unreliable source. Anything you want me to pass on?"

"Not necessarily. I'd like to ask for help but I know I can't, with the corporate liability and all."

"Sad, but true. Okay, I'll see you in a bit and if I get waylaid, save me some food for later. They should put a fruit bowl out or something for those who don't make the meal."

Amber shook her head. "I'm sure you won't starve, but I'll speak to Phil."

Nick grinned and then left the porch to go call Megan. Using the key, he opened the office, went to the desk phone, and dialed her cell. He wasn't sure if she would answer as it was still early morning, but he had promised to let her know what was happening.

"Hello?" Nick heard her husky morning voice and wished he was there lying next to her. Instead, he knew the dogs were keeping her company.

"Megan? It's me."

"Nick?" Megan suddenly sounded wide awake. "I waited for you to call back last night. What's going on? Did he show up?"

"No, he never did. The State Park Police will be here all morning. They'll be doing a search."

"Do you need volunteers?"

"No, we're not going to bring the public in on this yet. Maybe later if we don't find him. It's harder with volunteers involved. They'll start posting things on social media and a lot of negative press will be generated."

"Do you want me to come over? I could bring some food for the troops."

Nick had visions of Captain Davis hearing that Megan was involved and popping a gasket.

"No, Megan, you can't get involved. This is going to be a corporate liability. We can't have the public involved at all. If they need food, the camp manager, Phil, can make something for everyone. I just wanted you to know what was going on. I may not be able to call for a while, but just stay away from the park for now."

Megan was quiet for a bit. "If that's what you really want, then I will."

"I'm sorry Megan. It's not personal at all, but who knows what's going to happen. There will be a lot of police enforcement here today and it's best if you, and other civilians, are not involved in the mix."

"That does make sense," Megan conceded. "I'll stay away, but please keep me updated, as to what's going on, or at least let me know that you and Amber are safe."

"I promise I'll do that. We'll be fine. I've got to go now and get ready, but I'll keep in touch."

"Please, do that," Megan said with a sigh. "I miss you. I wish you were still here with me."

"I know," Nick said quietly. "I wish I was there too. I love you."

"I love you, too."

"I'll talk to you later." Nick smiled as he hung up the phone.

Walking around the desk, Nick locked the door and was on his way toward a hot shower and a scalding cup of coffee when he felt the satellite phone in his pocket start to ring. He grabbed the device and activated the phone. "Talk to me."

"Meet me on the red trail toward the marsh, fifty feet in." The line went dead. Nick recognized Luther's voice but knew he would want as little conversation as possible. Changing direction, Nick hurried toward the red trail and kept walking.

Deep into the path, he saw Luther step from the trees. Nick continued until he reached him. Getting straight down to business, Luther nodded and said, "We found your guy. He's dead."

"Damn. Seriously?" Nick could imagine the questions and accusations already.

Luther looked at him with a frown. "I brought some of the team. We split up on the paths. My red team spotted him but didn't touch anything. They confirmed he was dead and backed off. They checked his pulse with gloves, so no prints, no crushed fauna. I'm showing you where he is and then we're pulling out. I don't want anyone to know that my guys were anywhere near here, especially when the circus pulls into town."

"Circus? Why?" Nick watched Luther as he pondered the question.

"Your guy was murdered."

Nick was silent as Luther drew him toward a small clearing and then stopped. He pointed to a mound of leaves near the edge of a mucky waterway. "This is where I stop. You have to be the one to find him, so you can go in and secure the initial scene. We'll watch him while you call it in. Use the satellite phone while you're here. They couldn't track the registration if they tried. You won't see us, but we'll stay for surveillance until we see you and the police secure the scene. By the time that happens, we'll be out of sight and as far as anyone knows," Luther said with a pointed look, "We were never here."

"I thought you were retired military, emphasis on the retired," Nick said as he looked at Luther.

"As far as the government is concerned, the team no longer exists but there's nothing wrong with keeping in touch with some old buddies."

Nick knew there was more than that, a lot more, but he also knew when to keep his mouth shut. He turned and carefully stepped into the mucky ground near the marsh. The water may have been higher and receded recently. Enough to obscure evidence and change the debris field. He looked down at Felix Cooper. He was lying in a prone position, face down, head turned toward the side. His arms were to his side, fingers clutching wet, mucky leaves. Somehow, the fall-colored leaves seemed to emphasize the scene. His eyes were open but clearly seeing nothing, his mouth shaped in an expression of surprise. His bloody skull was caved in. Bits of bone and blood were splattered all over his back. There were flies and other bugs crawling through the scene and around his body. Nick also saw small marks on his face and body that could have been made from curious animals in the night, but he wasn't sure. Surely, animals would be attracted to the blood. He didn't see any personal items or effects or evidence of anyone else near the scene.

Turning, Nick realized he was now alone but knew Luther or one of his buddies lurked nearby, watching, close enough to secure the scene but out of sight. Nick stepped back on the main path and pulled out the satellite phone. The first call he wanted to make to report the death was to Captain Davis.

27

egan rolled over and let out a heavy sigh. She wanted to be with Nick, to help him, support him, and give him strength during the search for the missing executive, but she knew her presence would do nothing but emasculate him. He needed to regain his confidence, his strength, and his pride. The best way to help him accomplish that feat was to stay out of his way and his shadow.

Sitting up, she threw her legs over the side of the bed. Both Dudley and Bella crawled toward her, waiting to see if she was getting up for the day. Smokey was on the bed as well but stretched out near the opposite pillow. That cat believed she was royalty.

Megan soothed the dogs by petting them on the head and scratching behind their ears. As she did so, she cooed to them that everything would be fine, but wondered if she were trying to convince herself more than the dogs. Finally, she stood and walked toward the bathroom to start the day. Despite Nick's troubles, she had an appointment with Pastor Lee to discuss what they could do to best help the shelter and food pantry.

Looking in the mirror, Megan frowned when she remembered she had an appointment with Jonathan for dinner. She decided not to cancel as she felt torn between asking Jonathan and Teddy to help her make arrangements for the charity versus being available if Nick should need her help.

She dressed for the day and made her way downstairs to have coffee. After that, she planned on calling Teddy before she met with Marie and Georgie.

28

N ick took a few steps toward the parking lot and could see the State Park Police arrive in the distance. He had just hung up after listening to Captain Davis utter several expletives.

Nick watched as they parked their patrol vehicle near the edge of the parking lot. Two large officers exited the vehicle, adjusting their weapons and hats. Nick hadn't worked with the State Park Police in the past, but knew they were a progressive police department. They were sworn State Law Enforcement Officers and were certified under the Police Training Commission. Having the same law enforcement authority as all New Jersey municipal, county, and state police officers, they could arrest or detain anyone they considered suspicious, dangerous, or committing an offense in a state park, forest, preserve and all other designated state resources. However, their role in helping during environmental and public safety emergencies was crucial. They offered mutual aid assistance to all state and federal law enforcement agencies during threats and acts of terrorism. They had child abduction response teams and those that dealt with domestic violence on state ground. One main difference was they patrolled through rough terrain on foot, ATV's, bikes, boats, and motorcycles when necessary. They used K9 dogs, perhaps more extensively than other departments and they were used to dealing with natural terrain instead of city streets and freeways.

Captain Davis told Nick to keep him in the loop with the death investigation but had the good sense to let the State Park Patrol secure the scene. The State Park Officers turned as they heard Nick calling them. "Hey, down here." Nick waved at them until they got close enough for him to identify himself. His badge was on a chain around his neck. Nick watched the two officers trot toward him.

The first officer nodded his introduction. "Detective Wilson, and this is Officer Campbell."

Nick stuck his hand out. "Officer Nick Taylor, Misty Point Police Department. I'm here doing some private security for a retreat."

Detective Wilson nodded. "You've got a missing man?"

"Not anymore," Nick said. "I just found him this morning."

"And?" Wilson asked as Nick turned and walked toward the body.

"He's dead and it looks like he may have been murdered."

Nick walked the two men down the trail and then stepped back to allow them to examine the body.

After ascertaining the victim was clearly deceased, Detective Wilson called his base, while the other officer questioned Nick. "Has anyone else been out here?"

Nick shook his head. "Not that I'm aware of. The crime scene should be intact. I can't be sure if there were animals or anyone overnight. I had to stop searching when it got dark."

"What was different with your search this morning?" Campbell asked as he scowled.

"Different path, different lighting." Nick shrugged as he stared the officer in the eye. "I just found him and was in the process of contacting you and my commanding officer."

"And that would be?"

"Captain Davis of the Misty Point Police Department."

"We'll have to call the County Medical Examiner in."

Detective Wilson returned to where they were standing. "Reinforcement in ten minutes. They're calling in forensics. Have you contained the area?"

"I just found him and was attempting to notify the State Park Police when you pulled up. I haven't had a chance to do anything yet."

"Who's here in the park?" Officer Campbell asked.

"There's five executives in the cabin as well as a representative from the company that's sponsoring them."

"Name?" Detective Wilson asked as he took notes on a pad.

"Portal Health is the company," Nick replied. "There's also a camp manager they hired to cook for them and maintain bonfires."

"We're going to have to step back and go through the whole day again," Wilson said. "I'll need a timeline of exactly what went on yesterday, who was here and when the victim went missing."

Nick nodded as he organized his thoughts. They all turned when they heard sirens and activity in the parking lot. Within minutes, additional officers arrived at the scene. They were followed by a crime scene unit who pulled out biohazard suits and carried cases to collect forensic samples.

The first officer stopped when he saw Detective Wilson. "Everyone has been notified."

Detective Wilson nodded. "Close the park. Post someone at the entrance. Make sure no one comes in, especially the media, and make sure no one leaves."

"Yes sir," the officer said and ran out toward the parking lot.

29

Amber stood at the window and watched the activity outside. She hadn't heard from Nick. He never returned to the cabin to shower and change, and his breakfast tray was cold as it sat on the empty desk.

"What the hell is going on?"

Amber turned when she heard Dante's voice. "Felix never returned last night, so it's been reported to the police. Officer Nick Taylor is outside with other officers, but I'm not sure what department they're from or their specific plan this morning."

"What are we supposed to do?" Alberto Ortiz walked up beside them.

"I'm told we should go to the mess hall and have breakfast as usual. Someone will give us a bit more direction as to whether we'll hold lectures and our schedule."

"This is crap," Bob said as he approached the crowd holding his head. "Does anyone have aspirin? How is anyone supposed to sleep around here?"

Veronica frowned and reached for her handbag. She had an assortment of medication but was able to find an aspirin bottle and shake several into Bob's hand. She turned to Amber. "I have to do this several times a month at the office."

Amber raised her eyebrows as she watched him struggle with his hangover. Although she knew she shouldn't, she couldn't help expressing her thoughts. "Most people who enjoy nature do get up early to start activities and enjoy the morning air."

"Like hell," Bob said as he squinted toward the window and walked back toward his bunk. "I'm thirsty as hell and I've got to pee."

Amber heard a low laugh in her ear. She turned to find Veronica standing behind her. "That bastard deserves everything he gets. Too bad we can't bring more sunlight into the building."

"I agree you with there," Nancy Rogan said. "However, this whole retreat has been a waste of my time."

Amber raised her eyebrows and turned to the group. "Listen everyone, let's all head to the bathrooms and then mess hall. I'm sure someone official will come talk to us soon."

There was general grumbling and complaints as the surly group made their way out of the cabin. As they crossed the trail toward the other buildings, Amber was intercepted by her boss.

"Joe, what are you doing here so early?"

"It's a good thing I arrived early. They were just blocking the entrance. The police are not allowing anyone into the state park today," Joe Daman said angrily. "What the hell is going on?"

Amber shrugged. "As you know, Felix Cooper went missing last night, and he's not returned. They have the local police searching outside the park and I believe Nick met up with the State Park Police this morning to search inside the park. Beyond that, I have no details whatsoever. I was told to feed the crowd and wait for direction."

Joe Daman let out a string of expletives as he watched the executives come from the restroom and enter the dining hall. Amber and Joe Daman followed them in and saw several officers in the corner helping themselves to coffee and pastries. Joe rolled his eyes at Amber. "Now we're feeding the whole park?"

Amber shrugged as she looked at the man. She waited while the executives got in line, grabbed a tray, and walked past the window to get their breakfast. She followed them and made sure she was last in line for food. Right in front of her was Bob Flowers. After placing food on his tray, he went over to the coffee bar. When he realized the coffee carafe was empty, he tossed the carafe as well as his cup across the counter. "It's bad enough we must be in these deplorable conditions. Can we at least keep the coffee coming?"

Daman muttered under his breath as Amber hurried toward Bob. "I'm sorry. I'll make sure we fill the carafe right away. Why don't you have a seat and I'll bring the coffee to you? How do you like your coffee?"

"Hot with cream, lots of cream. I imagine you must have some. There must be a cow nearby."

Bob walked over to one of the tables as Veronica caught Amber's eyes and giggled.

Amber hurried into the back part of the kitchen holding the empty carafe. "Hi, Phil. Do we have more coffee?"

"It's perking. When I saw all the extra people in the park, I pulled out one of the bigger urns. I figure there's going to be a lot of activity today. The coffee is going to take another ten minutes."

"Good thinking," Amber said. "I'm sorry that you'll be busy but it's probably a good idea to keep the coffee, food and snacks coming. I'll try to get back here and help with clean up as soon as I can."

"I know you would, but I'll be fine. You just go do whatever it is you need to do with that crowd. Your job is going to be harder than mine."

Amber paused for a moment. "You're probably right, as long as I have a job."

They both looked up when they heard more commotion from the dining room. "I'd better go." Amber walked in to find that Nick and two other officers had come inside. She immediately walked to Nick's side. "What's going on?"

He turned and pulled her over to the corner. He purposely positioned himself toward the wall so no one could read his lips or face. "We found Felix Cooper."

"Great, right?"

Nick shook his head. "No, he's dead."

Amber immediately covered her mouth with her hands. "Oh no, what happened?"

"I can't say much and you're to keep this to yourself right now, but it appears he's been murdered."

Amber's face went from pale to ashen as the floor and ceiling swam before her. Nick grabbed her arm and steered her back into the kitchen and onto a chair. He gestured for the cook to bring him some cold water which he splashed on her face. "Amber, get hold of yourself. Put your head between your knees and breathe."

After a few moments, the color had returned to her face. "Nick, what the hell is going on?"

Nick shrugged. "I'm not at liberty to say. The Park Police will be making a statement to the executives. They will not be allowed to leave until everyone is questioned, and an initial investigation has started."

"They don't have a means of transportation anyway," Amber said. "And my boss said the park is closed."

"That's correct for now. No one in and no one out until the initial work is done. Any activity scheduled outside of the park for this group is cancelled."

She wiped her forehead with her hand. "This is awful."

"Yes, it is."

The swinging door burst open. "Amber? Are you in here? Where the hell is she?" Joe Daman swung around to find Amber and Nick in the corner. Beads of sweat still lined Amber's forehead as she steadied herself. "Why the hell aren't you out there? Our guests are complaining big time."

"Back off," Nick warned, as he outstretched a restraining arm toward Daman. "She's not feeling well at the moment."

"She's supposed to be calming the executives." Daman practically spit as he said the words. "She needs to be out there."

"We all need to be out there. The police will be making a statement shortly. Why don't you go first?"

The look of anger shot toward Nick was palpable, but Nick held his ground protecting Amber until Daman left. "That guy is an ass. I don't like him."

Amber moaned. "That should be my only problem right now."

30

M egan let the dogs out the front door and walked with them toward the beach. She knew it would be a long day and she'd jump every time the phone rang. She wanted to go to the state park and help Nick and Amber in any way she could. If she brought food or helped engage the guests, she knew her presence would land Nick in hot water if it was found out. He would be busy searching for the missing executive all day with other officers and personnel.

Megan looked up when she heard Dudley start barking. After a moment, she recognized Luther walking on the beach toward Misty Manor. Dudley and Bella ran toward him and wildly jumped as he threw a stick back and forth toward the water's edge. They continued to follow him until he approached Megan and walked her back to the house. They went up the front steps and stood on the porch.

"Luther, I'm so glad you're here. Nick is having trouble at the state park."

Luther's nod and intense eye contact made her stomach lurch. "Yes, I've come to fill you in."

Megan reached out and grabbed the rail. "Is Nick all right?"

Luther squeezed her upper arm. "Yes, he's fine. Don't worry about him."

"What then?"

"Have a seat for me, please?"

"It's that bad?"

Luther shrugged. "I don't know, but I'd rather you were sitting while we talk."

Megan took a seat in a dramatic fashion and then looked at Luther. "Okay, I'm seated. What's going on?"

Luther leaned against the rail on the front porch and crossed his muscled arms. "We found the missing executive this morning."

"That's great," Megan said. "Maybe that's why Nick didn't call me back."

"No, not exactly. Felix Cooper was dead when we found him, murdered to be exact."

"What? How? I can't believe it. Who would do something like that?"

Luther shrugged. "Could be anybody for any reason. You'd be amazed what people do these days. The point is he was murdered. I wanted you to know in case Nick doesn't get a chance to call you. There will be a lot of official action at that park today between officers, detectives, and forensics. Right now, they're not letting media or the public into the park, but I'm sure word will leak somehow. I didn't want you to hear it on the news and worry about Nick."

Megan looked stunned for a few minutes. She shook her head in disbelief. "Thank you, Luther. You know I would have panicked about Nick immediately, especially if I couldn't reach him."

"I know. I guarantee it'll be very difficult for him to step away and call. He'll have to make his own statement to the park police since he was acting security."

"Wait, do you think they'll try to make him responsible for this? How can one guy watch the whole park and multiple people at once?"

"I don't know what his role was. I guess it depends on what arrangements the company originally set up and their agreement with the local police."

"Oh no, how horrible. This was supposed to be a simple job for Nick to regain his confidence and make his way back to the force full time. Instead, he's going to go through hell from that company and his department. This is not going to go well."

"Don't worry, we have his back," Luther said. "Whatever it takes, we're there to support him."

Megan looked up at Luther. "I'm supposed to have a meeting today with Pastor Lee about the homeless shelter and food pantry. Later tonight, I was meeting with the foundation attorney to discuss what information we need to bring to the board. Do you think I should cancel those meetings? Will Nick need me?"

Luther shook his head. "Look, he's got a satellite phone he can use now. If he finds a minute to break away from that mess, he'll call. Until then, there is nothing you can do for him. The homeless shelter and food pantry are the best things to concentrate on so take the time to do what you need to do. You may not have time later if Nick needs you then."

"You're right," Megan said. "And if he calls me, I can step away from any of those meetings to talk with him. I'll go ahead then. I am so grateful you let me know about this and I won't say a word to anyone. You're right, I may have panicked if I heard it on the news."

Luther reached over and squeezed Megan's shoulder. "I know you'd do anything for Nick, but the best thing right now is to give him space. He'll call when he can and if I find out anything more, I'll let you know myself. In the meantime, you have my cell if you have any questions or concerns. Just give me a call or send a signal and I'll be here pronto."

Megan stood and gave Luther a quick hug. "Thank you for being such a great friend."

"Listen, I owe Nick my life and I'm ever thankful for that." Luther then gave a quick nod before he bounded off the porch.

Megan watched after him until the dogs came up the stairs. She reached down and patted their heads. "C'mon in the house. I've got meetings and we must stay on top of things in case Nick needs us today."

Amber, Nick, and Joe Daman assembled in the dining room along with Detective Wilson and Officer Campbell. They held a quick conference to discuss the talking points for the group and designate a speaker. Wilson was adamant that no extra or less information be revealed, and that no fact be changed until they had a chance to interview everyone that was in the park since the day before. The officers gauged the temperament in the room before they began.

Detective Wilson cleared his throat, "May I have your attention please?" The audience of executives became silent and looked up. It was apparent they had been complaining about their situation. "As you know, one of the executives, Felix Cooper, went missing yesterday. We are looking for any information that any of you may have about where he went when you were released on your free time. Perhaps he mentioned what trail he was taking or started out with one of you?"

"No idea, buddy," Bob Flowers said and sat back while crossing his arms. "Wouldn't that be what our security guard is here for?"

Nick took a deep breath before he spoke. "My role is supportive. None of you are under surveillance."

Bob muttered under his breath. "Guess that didn't work out so well, did it?"

Detective Wilson held his arms up in the air, trying to quiet everyone down. He raised his voice to be heard. "All right let's move on. We know that Felix works with Salacia Medical Supply. Does anyone know anything about his company? Did Felix talk to anyone yesterday? Did he mention any issues to any of you? This is the information we are looking for."

Nick and Amber watched as the executives made faces and looked down at their trays or out the windows. Detective Wilson continued.

"I will be meeting with each of you to see if you had any conversation or memories that would lead us in a particular direction for Felix. I will be taking you into a separate area to ask questions and then you can return to the mess hall for the next activity on your itinerary. Officer Campbell will be staying with you. We ask that you do not discuss this case with anyone, especially each other until you have met with me. Ms. Amber Montgomery and Mr. Daman can take this time to fill you in on the rest of your schedule until my interviews are complete."

"Shouldn't this retreat be cancelled at this point?" Veronica asked as she held her arms out wide. "Who's going to learn anything while you run around looking for a missing man?"

Detective Wilson quieted the group once again. "We are asking that none of you leave until we have more information. I believe the Portal Health Representatives will be in touch with your companies and make some sort of decision about the rest of the retreat but for now, you'll stay in the mess hall until we speak to you."

"We should be able to make a call to our company." Dante Valentino spoke up from his wooden table.

"No one is being held here. We are simply asking for help with some information. Thank you for being patient. We'll get this over with as soon as possible."

The small group gathered back near the kitchen. "You didn't tell them Felix was dead," Amber said quietly. "Was that purposeful?"

"Yes, we want to hear anything they may say. We'll let them know as a group that he's been found once I interview everyone. It's important to watch their reaction. I am trusting that everyone in this small group will respect that and keep all information confidential until we decide to release it."

"Of course," Amber said as she nodded.

Nick looked across the room and noticed that Joe Daman rolled his eyes. "What about their companies?"

"You're not to call them or release any information. We have detectives that will reach out to the family, Salacia Medical Supply, and their CEO, for further information once identity is confirmed. They need to do the official notification as well. In the meantime, you're to stay here with Officer Campbell and the rest of the group."

Static filled the air as Wilson was contacted on his radio. He walked a few feet away and quietly answered as he spoke into the microphone clipped to his shoulder. He then returned and quietly spoke to Nick. "They're asking for you to return to the crime scene. The county medical examiner is there and has some questions about your first view of the deceased."

"Of course," Nick nodded.

"In the meantime, everyone else will stay here. I'll be taking one guest at a time outside. The food manager can continue making coffee and food for everyone. Officer Campbell will be monitoring the conversation. Once again, not a word to anyone until I'm done."

"Got it," Amber said with widened eyes.

Wilson consulted a list and walked back to the group. "Would Alberto Ortiz please come with me?"

Nick turned toward Amber. "I'm going to head back then. I'll see you in a bit."

Amber watched as Nick, Detective Wilson and Alberto Ortiz walked out the door of the mess hall.

32

Megan pulled the dogs inside as she watched Georgie approach the house. They walked through the foyer to the kitchen. Marie had set out coffee and several plates, as well as a platter of bacon and bacon. On the side was a covered dish with toast and butter. "Good morning, everyone. I thought we could all use a good brunch before heading out to see Pastor Lee."

"This looks delicious," Georgie said as she pulled out a chair and sat. "I'm starving."

"That's because you run every day," Megan said. "You're burning all your calories."

"You could always come with me," Georgie said as she took several pieces of cheese from the plate Megan handed her.

"Perhaps I will, but I'll start by walking. You can run ahead and come back to find me," Megan said with a frown.

"I was waiting for Nick so I could help rehab him, but I guess he's tied up at that camp with Amber. They're probably having a great time. Sitting around the campfire, toasting marshmallows, playing music."

"I'm thinking not," Megan said as she bit into a piece of toast.

"Why not? You've heard from them?"

Megan fidgeted. "They have all those boring lectures scheduled. I'm sure it's not as much fun as you think."

"Nothing is easy these days," Georgie commented while they ate.

Marie collected the dishes and cleared the table. Within minutes the group was in the car and headed toward the shelter across town.

Pastor Lee was the senior pastor for the town church which was located near the beach. When he started his church in Misty Point, he began to serve an extra mass on the beach each day, near the water's edge. Although some in town were doubtful, the service proved widely popular. Many beachgoers, and others, who would not have physically gone to church, loved attending the beach mass. Spread around him on beach towels and chairs, beachgoers started their day with the early service and then enjoyed the gift of sun and sand for a while thereafter.

Many people flocked to the beach, as the power of the water made their problems seem miniscule, but having mass there as well seemed to help prioritize their issues. Soon after, the regulars, whether they were townspeople or young adults living off the beach for the summer, began to help whenever he needed assistance. A few brought guitars and musical instruments to the service and asked what he wanted them to sing and play to raise the spirit. The beach was always clean and the crowd respectful and helpful to others.

Pastor Lee never took a collection but left a basket near his side, which filled up regularly with donations. He used that money to start feeding young adults in need and arrange medical care, if needed. He collected clothing as well. He was sought out by others in town who needed assistance with food and were too embarrassed to ask.

Word spread around town and a few complaints were directed toward the mayor. His first response was to throw Pastor Lee and his mission out of town. However, others came to his defense as the ocean had always drawn troubled souls to the beach. The town did not have a formal food pantry or homeless shelter before his ministry. Many townspeople thought it was better to have an organized response for assistance and lessen petty theft and crime committed by those searching for food.

The mayor couldn't throw him out so he refused to provide aid, and the money Pastor Lee collected was not enough to meet the demand. The police could not assume responsibility, so all looked lost until Rose Stanford stepped in. It was her foundation which provided enough money, through a Stanford Grant, to purchase a respectable large building near the church. Anyone could find food, clothes, a hot shower, or an extra bed when needed. There were rules to follow, and the facility was constantly monitored. The shelter served a great purpose in town with very few problems.

Megan, along with Marie and Georgie, planned to meet with Pastor Lee to see how the foundation could continue to help. They pulled into the parking lot of the shelter and climbed out of the car. Pastor Lee was waiting for them inside.

33

Nick walked up to the site where Felix Cooper had died. The area was full of crime scene investigators collecting evidence, taking photographs, and measurements. Nick turned when he heard someone call out to him. The medical examiner, Dr. Chen, waved him over. Nick had worked with him on other cases and was glad he was assigned to this case, knowing he was thorough and would not sign off until he was sure he examined all evidence.

"Chen, how are you?" Nick extended his hand but then drew it back when he realized the pathologist was gloved, as well as wearing his hazmat suit.

"Good enough, I'm alive." Chen laughed at his own joke. "Hey, how are you doing? That last case was something with that poison."

Nick flushed as he didn't want anyone to think of him as infirm. "I'm coming along. I'm back from medical leave but I don't know what I stumbled into here. Captain Davis thought this might be an easy way to break back in."

"You still have symptoms?" Chen asked, his seriousness showing his concern.

Nick paused a moment. "Yeah, the right foot is a little numb, but my hair is growing back, and as you can see, my skin color is normal now. I'm wondering if the antidote was worse than the poison."

"You're alive, Nick. That's all that counts compared to this poor guy. What do you think happened here?"

"I'm not sure but I can give you a quick recap on yesterday."

"Great, let's start with that. I want to get some sort of timeline. Looks like the guy has been dead for approximately 18 hours according to the liver temp." Chen paused as a CSI tech handed him an evidence bag containing the bloody rock. He looked it over through the clear bag. "Definitely bits of hair, bone, and blood, but I'll be able to see a lot more at the lab. I don't know if we'll be able to recover any DNA from this. Bacteria tends to screw everything up. So, what happened yesterday?"

"It's straightforward. Everyone arrived, no one was happy, they had orientation, lunch and then had free time. Some went for a walk, one took a shower, one started drinking and two thought it was appropriate to hook up in the woods, but all that was over a period of four to five hours, so I don't have tracking of every person over that whole time. That's just the executives. There were hikers and other people in the park. It's a public state park and wasn't closed to the public yesterday."

Chen raised his eyebrows and nodded. "Do you know if the guy had anything expensive or flashy on him such as jewelry?"

"I don't think so," Nick said. "His wallet, phone and belongings are back at the cabin. He had a bird watching book there as well, so I don't think he had anything with him. I don't remember seeing him holding anything like that at lunch. Of course, I only was with him for a couple of hours."

"What about a camera? If he was a bird watcher, do you remember seeing a camera?"

"No, but that doesn't mean he didn't have one. He wasn't using his phone for that because he left it behind."

"Drugs? Do you think he could have been buying or selling? Meeting anyone in the park?"

"I didn't get the impression he had anything to do with drugs, but you never know, right?"

"Well, the tox screens will tell me that. Maybe I can get some info with a rapid today."

"I'm sure anything you find will help narrow things down." Nick shifted his stance to help his leg.

"Yes, but in the meantime, I'd like you to look over the crime scene with me." Chen walked closer to the body and pulled Nick behind him. "Let me know if the crime scene is as you remember it. Does anything look different? Think about the direction of his head, items surrounding the body and so on."

Nick walked up to the edge of the path with Chen. "I saw him this morning right after sunrise. Of course, he was clearly dead so I didn't touch him, and I tried not to step too near the body so I wouldn't ruin the trace field or any evidence. I had to run up toward the parking lot to attract the attention of the park police, but I was only gone a short while. We came back to the body immediately and waited until the troops arrived." Nick continued to look over the scene as he frowned. "His head was in that position because I remember looking at the dead eye. Flies were buzzing about his head and were attracted to that rock. I saw a dark substance on the rock and assumed it was dried blood. The only thing was there were a few scratches on his face, which I assumed may be animals through the night, but I don't know."

"The investigators will do their best to identify everything. Just checking if you saw anything else that would affect my findings. No drug paraphernalia? You'd be amazed what animals can drag away."

Nick shook his head. "No, no drugs, no personal effects, no phone. I saw him for the first time and was back here with the park police within minutes so there wasn't time for much to change after my first look."

"Okay, that wraps it up. We'll take him out now and back to autopsy."

"Let me know what you find?" Nick asked as he looked around. "Honestly, I'm not sure who's running the case from here."

Chen smiled. "The park police will use their own detectives, but I don't know who's assigned. Of course, we all help when needed. I'm sure the paperwork will find its way. Take care of yourself and I'll see you around, but not too soon, okay?"

Nick nodded as Chen gave him a wave and returned to the crime scene with final instructions to move the body to the morgue.

34

M egan, Georgie, and Marie walked into the shelter and spied Pastor Lee sitting at a reception desk in the front foyer. Megan immediately smiled and stuck her hand out.

"Pastor Lee, good morning. I'm sorry we're a few minutes late."

"No problem at all," he said as he stood and took her hand. "Megan Stanford, I'm so glad to meet you in person. Your grandmother was a wonderful person and talked about you while you were in college and then Detroit."

Megan felt a tug at her heart. She swallowed and continued as she gestured toward her companions. "I'd like you to meet Georgie Coles and Marie O'Sullivan."

Pastor Lee leaned forward and shook their hands. "Glad to meet you both. Why don't we go on a little tour and then all go to the conference area? Can I get you anything? Water, soda, coffee?"

"No, thank you," Megan said as the others agreed.

The group walked through the large one room building, which was separated into sections using furniture and discreet screens. There was an area with a small refrigerator and table to hold snacks.

"How many guests do you currently have?" Marie asked as she

opened the refrigerator door to find mostly bare shelves, except for bottled water and a protein bar.

"Only two now that the summer has ended. Most have moved on to other accommodations or were able to enter school or obtain a job. We were up to twenty-eight at one point during the summer. Thankfully, we had church members dropping off fresh food. That was a wonderful blessing, but I know I can't rely on them all the time."

"We're here to see how we can best help you," Megan smiled. "Why don't we take a moment to sit and discuss some details?"

"Of course, that would be most appreciated," Pastor Lee said as he led them toward the common area.

When the group was comfortably seated around the table, Megan started the conversation. "Pastor Lee, you know that my grandmother chaired the Stanford Grants, and your charity was one of which she fully approved. We would like to know how we can help you, but before we start, I want to say that Grandma Rose believed in donating things like materials, labor, kindness, and especially love. She would donate cash when necessary but since that didn't always reach the proper end point, she encouraged her charities to outline exactly what they needed, as well as their visions and goals."

The Pastor nodded. "I understand completely. We need clothes, food, and hygiene products. Let me explain. We often have guests, some who ran away from home, who do not have any possessions or belongings. We try to provide healthy food and clean, dry clothing. They are usually in need of personal products. We can always use extra bedding, sheets, pillows, and blankets."

Megan nodded. "I've always loved the idea of giving away hygiene packs, especially dental products. A good brush and toothpaste can usually ward off respiratory illness for some. Also, soaps, shampoos, conditioners, and so on."

"We can't give out razors until we assess the guest," Pastor Lee said. "I'm sure you can imagine why. You can't go wrong with a good comb or small brush. Once a person stays with us for a while, we ask them to help with chores. Kitchen duty, preparing food, washing dishes garbage and the like. Honestly, they do a great job and are happy to help, most of the time. If we have a guest that poses a problem or danger for others, we'll call the police for support. Any guest that stays more than three days or requests help will spend an hour or two with our social worker. The local hospital, Coastal Community, helps us out as well."

"It sounds like a great program," Megan said.

Georgie looked around the room. There were bunk beds, books, and some puzzles and games. "Do they respond to the social worker?"

Pastor Lee nodded as he looked at the trio. "Yes, some of the kids who seek help are sent by others who have stayed here in the past. Once they feel secure that we're not reporting them to the police or immigration, they relax and will work with us. If we're crowded, we try to have someone on site to provide security so there's no problem with petty crime or assault. Some have had enough exposure to domestic violence. Honestly, it's like any community. Most of the kids on the circuit, as we call it, know each other from other shelters and locations. Even though they're not together all the time, some have met or interacted with others at other places. Sometimes in a good way, sometimes not. We hope we always receive a good recommendation from someone that we've helped."

"That's fascinating. I'm going to be discussing the shelter with one of the foundation attorneys, tonight. We'd like to put together a proposal for aid including petty cash for emergencies, and supplies. Marie can help with the food pantry and organizing people to cook. She's phenomenal. She can help develop menus and a list of food staples, to keep on hand, and then fresh food and vegetables when needed."

Pastor Lee beamed. "This is so exciting. I'm feeling positive. I was worried about whether we'd have enough to support the shelter and I'd have to lose what we've gained so far."

"No worries there," Megan assured him. "Would you please do a small write up, outlining what you need and send it to me?" Megan took a business card out of her purse with the name Stanford Foundation on it. It also had her name as chairperson with a phone number, email and address. The corner of the business card had a small replica of Misty Manor and the lighthouse.

"Of course, right away."

"You can take a few days. I'll meet with the attorney tonight but then I'll bring the proposal to the whole board of directors for discussion next week."

Pastor Lee stood and shook each of their hands. "Thank you, thank you so much. I feel blessed and I send blessings with each of you today."

He walked the women to the door and waved to them until they got in their car and drove away.

35

Nick walked back toward the mess hall. Detective Wilson had spoken with several of the executives and was now secluded with the next, hoping someone would have seen or heard Felix say anything that would lead to a clue as to what happened.

Nick sidled up to Amber before he spoke. "What's up?"

"Nothing. We're all waiting for the interviews to be over. No one has left the mess hall and as far as I know no one knows that Felix is dead. Thank goodness we have a lot of coffee."

The door opened and Detective Wilson walked in behind Nancy Rogan. Neither one of them looked happy. She went over to grab a cup of coffee and Wilson approached Amber and Nick. "That's the last executive. I must interview your boss, Joe Daman. He doesn't seem happy about it."

"He's certainly not used to someone telling him what to do," Amber said.

"I didn't like the guy from the moment I met him. He's a bit of an ass." Nick looked at Wilson and shrugged.

"I'm sure I'll find out for myself in a few minutes. Once I'm done with him, I need to speak with each of you individually. Afterwards, we'll announce the death." Wilson turned to Nick. "Where do we stand with the crime scene?"

"Dr. Chen was done with his site exam. I believe they're in the process of removing the body now. They'll take him to the county morgue and do the post as soon as possible. Chen said he would do a rapid tox screen to see if anything showed up. I'm sure he'll be in touch with you."

Wilson nodded. "Good. It's better everyone stays here if they're doing the removal. We don't need any more confusion." He turned to Amber. "We'll have to talk about activities and your plans for the retreat once we finish speaking."

"That's up to Joe Daman," Amber said. "I'm not sure I'll have a job once we're all through with this."

Wilson nodded. "Okay, I'll bring Daman out and be back for you two. In the meantime, keep everyone here and no mention of the death."

"You got it," Nick said with a nod.

Wilson walked over to Joe Daman and pulled him outside. They could tell from his facial expression he was angry.

Nick turned to Amber. "Thinking about it, I remember seeing Daman on the porch, but I have no idea where he went when everyone went to eat lunch yesterday. Did he leave or did he come to lunch with us?"

"I have no idea, Nick. Joe popped in yesterday morning for which I was grateful because they weren't being very gracious or attentive. He helped get their attention and we gave our little cheer speech. I left with the guests to escort them to the bathrooms and the mess hall. Last, I remember, you were with Joe on the porch."

"Yes, we spoke for a few minutes and then I came to the mess hall to meet you. I remember him walking off the porch, but I'm not sure if he left the park. You and I had lunch in the mess hall, but I'm pretty sure Joe Daman didn't come in with us. The next time I saw him was when I came back to camp after searching and he was by the bonfire with you."

"He just shows up. We were sitting in front of the fire and suddenly he was there." Amber shrugged as she looked at Nick.

Nick spoke almost to himself. "Did he leave the park or just disappear? And if so, where did he go and why did he come back?" Nick thought for a few seconds and turned to Amber. "You said he didn't react when you told him Felix was missing."

"No, he didn't," Amber said as she thought about the day. "I was afraid he would be upset and blame me immediately, but he didn't react. He was rather quiet about it."

"Maybe he already knew Felix was dead, which is why he wasn't surprised when he turned up missing."

Amber's eyes opened wide. "You think so? Nick, that's a serious accusation. I'll admit he's a jerk and a womanizer, but I can't believe he's a killer. Why would he do that and why ruin his own retreat?"

Nick shrugged. "Murder is a strange thing. I don't think it was premeditated so who knows? Maybe something got out of hand. I know Daman's an uptight kind of guy. People kill others for many different and sometimes stupid reasons. Maybe the guy threatened to complain."

Amber bit her lip and shook her head. "Yes, Daman is high strung, but I sat near Felix Cooper during lunch yesterday. Quite frankly, compared to all the other guests, he was one of the most relaxed so I can't see him threatening to lodge a complaint."

"Interesting. I'll have to have a conversation with Wilson when we're together. Hopefully, he'll ask Daman where he was yesterday afternoon."

"Hey, how long do we have to sit in this dump?" Bob Flowers was walking toward Nick and Amber. "Are we being held prisoner or what? Forget my company, I'm calling my attorney as soon as I can get to a phone."

Nick held his hand up. "Back off buddy. The lady is only doing what she's been told to do by her boss."

"This is harassment," Flowers yelled. "Are we being charged with something or what? I don't understand what the hell is happening around here."

The others watched from the tables but started shouting comments toward Nick and Amber, clearly showing their disgruntlement.

They all turned when the door opened, and Wilson reappeared with Joe Daman. Wilson walked up to the group. "What's the problem?"

Bob Flowers made a rude gesture. "How about if you tell us? We're being held here against our will. What's going on?"

Wilson appeared to think for a moment and then took off his hat. "Okay, everyone come close and listen up." He waited until everyone had gathered close enough to hear him, but in that way, he could more easily watch their reaction.

"Mr. Felix Cooper has been found."

"Great, then we can get the hell out of here," Bob Flowers said as he stood up. "Why are we still here?"

Wilson looked down at the floor for a moment, then looked at the group with his lips pursed before he announced, "because he was found dead."

"What?" Veronica asked, her eyes wide in surprise. "How? Why?"

"Obviously, if we had those answers, we wouldn't be asking a lot of questions," Wilson said as he put his hat back on. "The coroner has come and collected his body. We're waiting for the preliminary results to get some answers regarding his cause of death. If anyone here would like to change any of your answers to our little interview, please let me know."

"Why us?" Nancy Rogan asked. "Are you concentrating on this little group? There were other people in and out of the park."

"Point taken," Wilson said. "We will be interviewing everyone about their whereabouts since they arrived yesterday. I'm not saying that anyone here is the killer, but someone may have information that may be important. Perhaps you don't realize you saw him walk off in a certain direction yesterday or you may remember a comment he made during lunch."

Dante Valentino spoke up. "Although I would not readily admit this at work, I was taking photos of the camp yesterday. I've got some friends that are into extreme exercise. I thought we could get something together another time."

"I'd like to take a look at those photos if you would hand over your phone," Wilson said.

"Sure, but my phone is back at my bunk so it will have to be after this."

"Make sure it happens," Wilson said as he gave a pointed look at Dante. He then turned to Amber and Nick. "I need to ask questions of both of you. Amber, you can help your guests back to the cabin and bathrooms, but no one is to leave the camp. You're not being held but we would like everyone to stick around until we have a little more information. I'll speak with Mr. Daman about next steps."

"Well, wait a damn minute here," Veronica said. "You never explained how Felix died. Did the man have a heart attack or is there a crazed killer on the loose at camp?" She groaned and threw back her head. "It sounds like the plot of a typical horror movie."

"I'm not at liberty to say at the moment," Wilson said. "It's an ongoing investigation. When we have more details and I hear from the medical examiner, I'll be able to make a statement to all. In the meantime, the man died on state property, so we must investigate just like any other unexpected death."

"Are we safe here?" Alberto Ortiz spoke up for the first time.

"You are in the safest position you could be right now," Wilson said. "We don't know what happened but if you stay together as a group, you'll be fine. There are currently more officers in the park than out, so this is the best place to be." Wilson looked at Nick and Amber. "Let's switch this up. Officer Taylor, why don't you escort these fine guests to the bathrooms and the cabin. They are to stay in the camp, and we are to know where they are at all times. I'll take this opportunity to speak with Amber Montgomery and then you two can switch."

Nick gave a curt nod and extended his arm to usher everyone out of the mess hall and toward the bathrooms.

Amber watched as they all filed out. She turned when she heard

Wilson's voice in her ear. "Ms. Montgomery, if you would come with me, please?"

"Of course," she said as she followed Wilson out another door.

36

Megan was greeted by the dogs as soon as the women stepped into the foyer of Misty Manor. They dropped their purses on the table and made their way into the kitchen. As Marie pulled food out of the refrigerator, Megan brought glasses and iced tea to the table.

"What did you think of the shelter and Pastor Lee?"

"The shelter looks like a great place for people in need," Georgie said. "Years ago, we would have kids with no place to stay camping out on the beach all summer. When Pastor Lee opened the shelter, they had a safe place to go and were able to leave the beach. I mean, the beach is great to visit but these kids needed a safe place with good food."

Marie walked over with a plate of sandwiches. "I love the food pantry. I think your instincts were exactly right, Megan. We need to stock those shelves with staples and then provide fresh food during the week when there is need. I can't wait to start working with them on that. I could bring over cooked food when the shelter is particularly full."

"But it would be better if you could cook there," Megan said. "I wonder if we would need a permit from the town to add better kitchen facilities."

"Don't hold your breath if the mayor has anything to do with it, especially if he knows the kitchen will be financed by the Stanford Foundation," Marie said.

"I agree," Georgie said. "At some point, Mayor Davenport has got to go."

"Let's not get ahead of ourselves," Megan said as she poured the iced tea.

"What about dinner tonight?" Marie asked. "Are you still going out with Jonathan?"

Megan pursed her lips as she pondered the question. "I need to talk to Teddy first. I didn't reach him earlier. Honestly, I'm torn between staying home, in case Nick calls for something, and making arrangements for the shelter." Megan looked up at Marie. "Either way, don't cook for me tonight. If I don't go out with Jonathan, I'll grab something somewhere."

"Hmmm," Marie said. "That's the problem, who's going to grab you?"

Megan and Georgie both laughed at Marie's concern.

"Go ahead and laugh but I'm afraid that boy has ulterior motives or even if they're just genuine feelings, you have Nick to think about."

"Believe me, Marie, Nick and Amber have been on my mind constantly, especially since I've heard there's trouble at the camp."

"Trouble? They're having trouble. What's going on?" Georgie turned to Megan as she waited for an answer.

Megan hesitated for a few moments while she decided how much to tell them. "Nick was able to slip into the camp office and give me a quick call. From what I understand and believe me I do not have the whole story, one of the executives who arrived for the retreat disappeared after lunch on Sunday. The police were called, and they were searching for him."

"What do they think happened?" Georgie asked.

Megan shrugged. She hoped her face didn't give away the fact that she knew more of the story.

"I haven't heard from Nick or Amber since then. They don't have any service and from what I understand there was to be State Park Police conducting search and rescue all day."

"I hope they're okay," Marie said. "Do you think they need anything?"

Megan shook her head. "As a matter of fact, Nick told me the park was now closed to the public and I was to stay as far away as possible. He wanted me to know what was happening in case something leaked out on the news."

"You're still going out with Jonathan then?" Marie asked as she tilted her head forward.

"I think so unless Nick calls me. I haven't been able to reach Teddy and I don't want to make Pastor Lee wait so I might as well get this over with."

"Just as long as you make your boundaries clear with this boy," Marie sniffed.

Megan grinned as she nodded. "Yes, I'll be a very good girl."

37

Nick turned to see Amber walk into the cabin. She had spoken with Detective Wilson for forty-five minutes answering questions about the program, her boss, the executives, and the timeline for Sunday's activities. "That was somewhat grueling," Amber said. "I've never been questioned by the police about anything."

"It's just protocol, Amber. They'll ask everyone the same questions and compare answers. If anyone is really off the mark, they'll reinterview to see if they want to change their statement. Many people seem to forget certain items, or their recollection suddenly has more clarity when they're confronted with information."

"Interesting," Amber said as she nodded.

"Let's take our friend Dante over there," Nick said. "I reminded him that Detective Wilson wants those photos from his phone, but he's saying he hasn't had time to check them yet. I have a feeling he took a few photos of his tryst with Veronica in the woods and wants to delete those before anyone else looks at his phone. Who knows what else could be in his photo library?"

Detective Wilson opened the screen door of the cabin and wagged a finger at Nick to come join him. Nick turned to Amber. "I've got to talk to Wilson. The group has been talking, arguing or in general trying to make sure I'm not involved in their business. Keep an eye on them."

"Will do," Amber said as she watched Nick walk out.

Amber turned toward the group and tried to engage them. It was now getting toward late afternoon and not much had been accomplished. The sun went down at 7:00 p.m. in October. The lectures planned for the first day were never delivered and Joe Daman had disappeared while Amber was with Detective Wilson.

Dinner would be served in another hour or two and the fire would start at dark. "Hey, how is everyone feeling?" They turned and looked at Amber, but no one spoke. Amber smiled and tried to be helpful. "I'm sorry we didn't get to start our lecture series today. We have a lot of activities planned for the week. In addition to speaking about our customers and how our products make a difference in their daily lives, we had a few trips scheduled to see that in action. Today's schedule was to be a nursing home located in Misty Point and Coastal Community, a hospital where various doctors planned to speak with you. We also wanted you to tour the local shelter for the homeless to see how we support the community."

Alberto Ortiz raised his hand. "Depending on what happens, I would still be interested in some of those trips."

"Oh, wow. You've got to be kidding me," Veronica yelled. "A man died here today."

"Yes, but we don't know how yet. Perhaps he was hiking and had a heart attack." Alberto raised his shoulders.

"Probably not if all these cops are still around," Bob Flowers yelled from his bunk. Dante shook his head and finally went to his bunk, retrieved his phone, and slipped it into his pocket. He was about to say something to Amber when Nancy Rogan spoke out.

"Listen, I hate to crush happy hour, but I'd really like to go to the bathroom and then take a shower. We've been practically held hostage in one building or another today. If we're not being charged, I want a shower."

"Well, I, ah....," Amber hesitated as she looked at the group.

"The detective said we couldn't leave the camp, but he didn't say we had to stay in the cabin," said Bob Flowers. "I agree, time to get some fresh air."

Amber saw him sneak a flask into the pocket of his jacket.

"I can't stop you from going to the bathroom," Amber said as she looked at the various executives.

"Damn straight," Nancy said as she gathered up a few towels and clean clothing. She then brushed right by Amber, knocking her shoulder as she did so. Amber stepped back a few feet as the other executives followed her. When Amber ran onto the porch, she saw them heading for the bathrooms. She looked for Nick and Detective Wilson as she didn't know what to do. *Stand outside the bathrooms? Spy on their most private moments?*

Wringing her hands, she flew off the porch looking for Nick. Amber quickly moved to the back of the mess hall. She wanted to check the covered pavilion where she knew Detective Wilson was conducting his interviews. She needed to find them and ask what she should do with the executives since they walked out of the cabin in protest.

38

Megan tried once more to reach Teddy, but he didn't answer. Perhaps he was in court for the day or out of town. He didn't have to leave his schedule with Megan, but she wasn't sure if he knew she was scheduled to have dinner with Jonathan. Megan realized that Teddy made the final decisions, and he wanted Jonathan to learn about the foundation. Megan hoped that Jonathan would relay all her thoughts to Teddy so they could present a solid front at the board meeting. In addition, she thought it was high time she was involved in the final decisions as well. At any rate, she would have dinner with Jonathan and give him the facts to bring back to Teddy.

She took a shower and picked out a dress she had recently purchased while shopping with Amber. As Megan held the dress up to herself in the mirror, she was struck with a sad feeling that she hadn't been able to wear it to dinner with Nick.

Between the end of summer and his rehab from being poisoned, they had stayed close to Misty Manor. It was those six weeks that brought her closer than ever to Nick. Caring for him, making him eat, and seeing him vulnerable, made her love him more. She realized he wanted to get back to his life, but she still felt a bit stung when he jumped at the chance so quickly.

To be sure he hadn't called, she checked her cell phone again. She was thankful that Luther had clued her in, but now worried that Nick still hadn't found time to call. She hoped Luther was there, watching over him and the camp. Worries about Nick and Amber came to her mind, and she would have no problem turning them into mental disasters if she let herself dwell on them. Facts, she needed to stick to facts. Nick would call as soon as he could, and the gang would all be back at Misty Manor celebrating soon.

Megan looked at the mirror to make sure she was happy with her clothing choice for tonight's dinner but then stopped and decided to turn on the local news to see if there was any information about the camp.

39

"Have you been able to contact family?" Nick asked Detective Wilson as he sat across from him in the pavilion. They had spent a good bit of time talking about Nick's assignment and his observations from the day before. Wilson also asked about his first impression of Felix as well as others staying in the camp.

"I haven't personally talked to Felix's family, but one of our detectives drove to North Jersey to do the death notification. She's very good and will try to elicit any information she can once they've been notified. Sometimes a family will want to talk to help process what's happened."

"Been there," Nick nodded. "How about the company he worked for?"

Detective Wilson looked at Nick. "In the spirit of cooperation, I'll answer some of your questions, but I don't have to tell you this information is privileged."

Nick was quiet as he looked at the detective. He understood it didn't look good for him to be anxiously asking too many questions. The State Park Detective was running the investigation and knew his stuff. Perhaps he could sense Nick's anxiety or guilt about the dead man.

"As I said, we're currently contacting the family to make the notification. We're contacting the company to ask about his behavior and his feelings about the retreat in general. We're running a criminal background check on our guy as well as prints and the works. One of our officers are pulling any video they can find of anyone coming in and out of the park. As a matter of fact, we think we got the plate of the car the hikers drove in here yesterday. We've got someone checking on them as well." Wilson put on his hat and nodded at Nick. "I can understand your interest, seeing as how this is your first assignment with the department, after medical leave."

Nick raised his eyebrows and turned to Wilson who replied. "Yeah, we had to check up on you too. That's the job."

"Nick, Nick, Detective Wilson." Both men turned as they heard Amber calling out to them as she rounded the corner of the mess hall on the run. She was breathless when she reached the pavilion.

"Amber, are you okay?" Nick stood up and held her by the shoulders as she took deep breaths. "What's wrong?"

"I had to find you both right away. I didn't know what to do and I'm afraid of doing exactly the wrong thing."

"Calm down," Detective Wilson said. "Why don't you start with telling us what's happened?"

"I was in the cabin with the executives. I guess they play a lot nicer when you're around, Nick, since you're an officer. They started getting snarky with me about being held hostage and said they weren't going to stay there. They said they were allowed to leave the cabin if they didn't leave the camp. Then they grouped together, pushed me aside and all stomped out."

"Where are they now?" Nick asked.

"That's just it. I don't know and I either had to follow them or come find you. Some went toward the bathroom. One or two went toward a hiking trail." Amber sighed and shook her head. "I don't know where anyone is. I'm so sorry."

"Let's get out there," Wilson said as they started walking toward the middle of the camp.

40

Dante Valentino sat on a large rock in the middle of the woods behind the main cabin. After they all walked out, he visited the bathroom and then the woods to look at his phone for photos of Felix Cooper. He didn't want to hand the phone over until he had a chance to see what else may be on it. Perhaps if he located a photo, he could simply text that one to the police officer that was babysitting the group or the Detective.

He heard someone walk up behind him but didn't turn right away as he was scrolling through photos. "Hey, I was hoping you would meet me here. I'm looking through my photos." He stopped, located the photo he remembered and held the phone so the person behind him could see the photo. "I found it. Can you believe it? I found the photo. Look at the two of them walking off together. Man, if Felix saw the look on that person's face, he would not have walked into the woods. Talk about turning to stone. No wonder he wound up dead." Dante felt a hand on his shoulder. "You see this? I've got to see if I can find Nick what's-his-name so I can send this photo. Hey, are you okay?"

He finally turned his head to see the person behind him. "Oh, it's you. I was expecting someone else to meet me here."

Dante was not fast enough to block the blow to his temple. He fell to his knees, nausea and dizziness threatening to overwhelm him as he tried not to throw up. He spit out phlegm, and said, "Here, take my phone. I don't need to show anyone. You take it and do whatever you want with it. I swear my lips are sealed about this. That photo isn't proof of anything, just a random photo."

Dante took a deep breath as his phone was snatched from him. A bit shaky and nervous he took another deep breath. He felt a hand on his shoulder again but didn't react until he realized there was now a vine wrapped around his neck. He quickly put up his hands to grab and pull the vine loose, but it was too strong for him to break. As the tension grew tighter, he started having trouble breathing. His vision became pinpoint in front of his eyes, and he quickly grew light-headed. After a minute, his hands dropped from the vine around his neck and his eyes rolled back in his head. To be sure of a result, the vine was wrapped several more times around his neck and pulled tighter until all signs of life were gone.

When the tension on the vine was released, his body dropped to the ground. His open eyes saw nothing of what was in front of him as his killer and phone both faded away into the brush.

41

M egan still had a little time before Jonathan picked her up for dinner. She gathered the dogs and walked out to the porch to watch the ocean waves roll onto the beach. Low tide ensured calm waves this evening, which was perfect, as she needed to clear her mind. Pulling the rocker toward the stairs, she sat as the dogs ran down and sniffed the scrub. They stopped and stared at something on the side of the house. Neither dog barked but stood at full attention which caused Megan's stomach to knot as she waited to see what had caught their eye.

A man walked forward and with a wave of his hand, the dogs broke free and ran to the water's edge. Megan jumped up from her chair and turned.

"Megan, how are you this evening?"

"Luther? I didn't recognize you right away. I wasn't sure why the dogs had stopped running."

"Sorry, I didn't mean to frighten anyone."

"That's okay. I guess I'm jumpy this evening. Apparently, my dogs have been completely trained by you."

Luther laughed at her comment.

Megan looked worried. "I haven't heard anything from Nick. Have you?"

Luther climbed the stairs and rested on the porch railing. "No, I haven't. I dropped by to see if you'd heard anything. I knew the park would be busy today dealing with the death, but I imagine that investigation would have slowed down by now."

"He hasn't called all day," Megan said as she sat down in the rocker. "I hope everything is okay. Have you been back there at all?"

Luther shook his head. "No, I knew there would be detectives and officers hanging around. Not that they would have seen me, but I didn't want to add to any activity over there."

"Do we have any way to contact Nick?"

"Actually, I do," Luther said as he reached into his pocket. "I know there isn't any service over there, but I dropped off a satellite phone this morning, strictly for emergencies. He knows not to use it in front of anyone. I didn't want to call him, not knowing who he was with."

"Is there a way we can try?"

Luther stood and stared at the ocean. The dogs were running in and out of the waves as they broke on the shore. The sky was beginning to turn various colors, as the day began to wind down.

"I can send a signal. If Nick is available, he may be able to call. We can give it a try."

"Please? I'd feel better knowing he's okay, even if he's just busy."

Luther pulled a small phone out of his pocket. He hit a few buttons and placed the phone on the rail. He then shifted position and continued to stare at the water. "Okay, now we wait. If he received the signal, which he probably did, he'll call back when he's free."

"What's wrong Luther? I've never seen you look so upset." Megan stood up and walked to the edge of the porch. "Is there something you're not telling me about what's going on?"

Luther shook his head. "No, you know what I know. We'll wait a little bit. If we don't hear from him soon, I'll be in the park tonight and find out what's happening myself."

42

Detective Wilson, Nick and Amber rounded the mess hall. Off to the side, they spied Bob Flowers playing horseshoes with Alberto Ortiz.

"For some reason, that's a sight I never expected to see," Nick said. "But where are the others?"

"I could check the ladies' room," Amber said. "Maybe Nancy and Veronica are there."

"Together?" Nick raised his eyebrows. "I don't see that happening either, but who knows? I'll go check the cabin. Let's meet back here in ten minutes and reorganize."

Detective Wilson looked at his watch. "I'm going to take that time to check in with our unit. I want to see if we have any word from the victim's family or work. You two okay with that?"

"We've got it," Nick said. "We'll meet you back here as soon as you're ready."

"Great, appreciate it," Wilson said as he turned and headed toward his car in the parking lot.

Nick gestured toward the bathroom as he spoke with Amber. "Let's go. Just pinpoint where everyone is and then we'll meet back.

Don't try to engage them other than any questions they may have. We just have to keep track of their movements."

"You got it, boss." Amber gave a mock salute and headed toward the bathrooms while Nick strode off toward the cabin. She opened the wooden door and winced as the spring hinge squealed in response. A shower was running but Amber heard or saw no one in the bathroom. She quickly walked back and forth in front of the toilet stalls and noticed the door was open. No one was inside. Thankfully she didn't have to bend over to look for feet in each stall. Amber tried to be as quiet as possible. She walked over toward the shower stall and called out. Pulling open the door and invading someone's privacy without a strong excuse would not be tolerated at this point.

"Hello?" Amber held her breath and waited for a few minutes but heard no reply. Swallowing, she tried again. "Hello? Is anyone in the shower?" Within a minute, the shower stopped running and Amber heard a woman softly cursing.

"Hello? Who's in the shower? This is Amber. I'm checking to see if you need anything."

Amber jumped when the door was suddenly yanked open several inches. Veronica was standing there in a towel. "I'll tell you what I need. A shower with hot water that will last more than five minutes. These damn push knobs only give you a couple minutes of cold water and I don't want to have to push the damn thing twenty times to take a decent shower."

"I'm sorry. I wanted to make sure you were okay."

Veronica continued to complain as she wrapped a towel around her head and pulled the one around her body tighter. She pointed her finger at Amber and yelled. "Let me tell you something. My shower, in my luxurious apartment in Manhattan, has a complete panel tower system with multiple body jets and a rainfall shower head with hydro powered LED lights that change according to the temperature of the water. I come here and I'm lucky to get five minutes of cold water using some disgusting push knob that has caked dirt and leaves on it. I can't wait to get out of this hell hole and back to my apartment."

"Wow," Amber nodded. "I didn't even know they made showers like that."

"You better believe it. There's a whole world of comfort and excess out there and if I wanted to live in a forest, I would have permanently moved to one."

"Noted." Amber pointed toward the door. "Well, I'm going to give you some privacy and go. I wanted to make sure everyone was okay. Dinner will be ready soon and we want to make sure everyone is as comfortable as possible."

Amber ducked at the towel thrown at her head. She then scurried back to the door and into the clearing to meet Nick who was striding toward her from the cabin.

"Is anyone in the bathroom?"

"Veronica was the only one in the ladies' room. What about the cabin?"

"Nancy Rogan was in there reading a fiction novel. I didn't see Dante."

"Maybe you should check the men's room," Amber said with a shrug. "I didn't go in there."

Before Nick could reply, his pant pocket started to beep.

"What's that?" Amber asked looking around.

Nick searched the area before he answered. "It's a satellite phone."

"Where did you get that?"

"Luther left it for me yesterday morning," Nick said. "We didn't want anyone to know I have it or a connection to him. Do you see Wilson anywhere?"

Amber looked around. "No, I don't see anyone except Bob Flowers and Alberto playing horseshoes."

Nick pulled Amber by the arm as he walked toward the back of the mess hall. Grabbing the phone out of his pocket, he quickly pushed reply. He waited a moment until the phone was answered.

"Luther?" His voice was hushed and quiet.

"Can you talk? Are you alone?" Luther asked.

"I'm with Amber. We're alone now but Wilson will be back any minute."

"Status?" Luther asked not wanting to mince words or waste time.

"Wilson questioned everyone in the park. The natives are getting restless and agitated. They staged a walk out from the cabin and we're trying to find them all now."

"The victim?" Luther asked.

"Waiting for Chen's report. They're contacting his family and work."

Megan grabbed Luther's arm, pleading for the phone. He relented and handed it to her with raised eyebrows sending a warning.

Megan nodded before she put the phone to her ear. "Nick, are you and Amber, okay? Do you need anything?"

Nick swallowed hard for a second, surprised at the emotion welling up. He realized how serious the situation had turned. He nodded, blew out a breath and said with a thick voice, "We're fine. We'll be okay."

"I'll be quick but today Pastor Lee had said certain groups all tend to know each other. I was thinking, if you give me the names of the guests, I can do some research for deeper ties. I'm an investigative reporter, Nick. I can help."

"You know I can't do that, Megan." Nick said as he glanced at Amber. He gestured with his chin toward the front of the mess hall. She quickly looked out front and shook her head to let him know Wilson was nowhere in sight.

Luther nodded at Megan for the phone. Megan quickly shouted into the phone. "I love you, Nick. Tell Amber we're praying for everyone."

"Me too, Megan."

She gave the phone back to Luther who quickly spoke to Nick. "I'll be in your neck of the woods tonight. Listen for the owl." Luther hung up the phone and disconnected the call.

Nick stuck the device in his pocket mere seconds before he heard a voice. "There you are." He and Amber turned and saw Wilson walking toward them.

"Do you think he heard or saw us?" Amber asked under her breath.

"I doubt it," Nick said. "But let's keep it our little secret."

43

L uther closed the phone and looked at Megan. She was nervous she would be scolded for speaking to Nick, but she needn't worry.

"That's a good idea you pitched," Luther said.

"What does it matter? He wouldn't give me the names." Megan looked down at the beach to make sure the dogs were still playing nearby.

"He can't give them to you, but I can." Luther watched her as he spoke.

"You know who's at the retreat?" Megan turned toward him.

"I'll find out. I have a man who can get that information. I'll pass the names to you. Maybe we can help more with research than anything else at this point."

"I was with Nick yesterday morning in the parking lot," Megan said with a small laugh. "I can't believe it was just yesterday morning. It feels like it's been a month since I dropped him off."

"Did you see anything specific? Do you remember anything?"

"Yes, we were watching the cars dropping off the guests. There are three executives from Manhattan. It was odd because two were in one car, a man and woman. Another man arrived by himself, but Nick was guessing their identities from the license plates. Those three guests were in cars with New York license plates. I think he said the company was Antacus Pharmaceuticals."

"That's great," Luther said. "Half the work is already done."

"I know there are three more guests, and they are all from companies in New Jersey."

"Interesting and you're completely right. Executives all travel in small circles, and they may know each other from different times and places."

"I can do some computer work and I still have a couple of places to search that aren't out there for the public. Just get me all the names. I can start with the pharmaceutical name but that would be hard to narrow down." Megan's excited voice showed hope.

"Just remember we don't know if the killing was random or done by another executive. We have no motive. We don't have enough information to draw any conclusions at this point."

"We do have a starting point. I have to go out with Jonathan tonight for the foundation," Megan said as she looked at her watch. She didn't see Luther raise his eyebrows and he remained silent. "I'll try to rush through dinner and the proposal and get back as soon as I can. You get me those names and I'll start searching immediately. I'll have Marie put a large pot of coffee on to get me through the night."

Luther nodded. "Okay, I'll be in touch." He squeezed her arm, turned, and left the porch. Megan called the dogs and stared after Luther as he quickly disappeared into the night. She didn't know all his background or training, but she was glad he was on their side.

44

W ilson approached them as he asked, "Okay, so what do we have going on here? Where Is everyone?"

Nick turned and pointed toward the horseshoe pit. "Bob Flowers and Alberto Ortiz are over there. Veronica is taking a shower in the bathroom and Nancy Rogan is reading a fiction novel in the cabin. I was about to go to the men's room to see if I can find Dante Valentino. We haven't located him yet."

"Let's check the bathroom," Wilson said. "Otherwise, we have a rabbit. He could have run because he's the killer or because he's a target, but either way, if he's not in that bathroom I'm calling in search and rescue with the dogs."

"What's going on?"

Amber jumped as Nick and Detective Wilson turned to see Joe Daman standing behind them.

"How is it you show up at the most inopportune times," Wilson snapped. "Where have you been and how the hell did you get in here?"

Daman bristled. "I've been trying to get information from my company files about these executives and, no thanks to you, I've had to hike in and out of this park several times over."

"What didn't you understand about no one in or out?" Wilson demanded.

"Listen, I'm responsible for this retreat so I'll do whatever I have to do to keep everything from caving in." Daman turned to Amber. "I want you to set up a damn lecture for the retreat as soon as possible."

"It's almost dinner time," Amber said. "Can we have the first lecture tomorrow morning?"

"Hopefully, we'll be able to reclaim our retreat and make that happen," Joe said as he glared at Wilson.

Wilson nodded with a tight smile. "Well now, Mr. Daman, that all depends on whether we find your missing guest, now, doesn't it?"

"We found him," Daman yelled turning to Amber.

Amber shrugged. "Sorry, but right now we can't find Dante Valentino."

Daman's face turned red. "What the hell are you talking about?"

Wilson's grin widened. "That's right and if Nick and I don't find him in the bathroom, we're bringing in the search and rescue dogs. So, you can have whatever lecture you'd like but you'll have to work around the officers in the park. No one else is to leave."

Daman's mouth opened and his color turned darker as he raged. "How did you lose another guest?"

"I've been busy interviewing witnesses and collecting information from my men," Wilson stated coolly. "But I think I'm going to have another sit down with you, Mr. Daman."

Amber watched Daman's color turn purple. Trying to defuse the situation, Nick stepped in front of Joe Daman and looked at Wilson. "Did anything come out of the notification with Felix's family or work?"

Wilson dropped his laser focus on Daman and looked at Nick.

"No, his parents were understandably upset. There's no girl-friend, wife, or friends in the picture that he would be trying to meet. His manager at his place of work, Salacia Medical Supply, said he was looking forward to the conference even though he didn't volunteer to attend so he was one of the only executives here whose attendance wasn't critical. It certainly doesn't sound as if he was meeting anyone or looking for trouble and his death doesn't sound like a targeted hit."

Nick nodded while Amber tried to calm her boss down.

"What about the hikers from yesterday. Do we know who they were?"

Wilson nodded. "We got lucky on that one. A camera caught the car license plate, so we were able to track them down today. Two hikers, who visit on a regular basis, were here yesterday to follow the Pine Trail, which is approximately eight miles long. I've got a detective meeting them to see if they happened to notice anyone or anything unusual in the park."

Nick nodded and blew out a breath. "No thread to pick up on yet?"

"We're working on it, Officer Taylor. We're still digging information for the executives as well as the camp manager for that matter."

Nick nodded. "Things can run slow."

"You, however, appear to have been fully cleared so let's go check out the bathroom for this Valentino fellow." As they walked away, Wilson looked back at Daman and whispered to Nick. "I'm going to investigate that guy a lot deeper. I don't like him and he's always around when he's not expected."

"Good, I don't like him either," Nick agreed as the two men trudged toward the bathrooms.

45

Megan dressed as she readied for dinner. She wanted to get it over with so Jonathan could start working on the objectives with Teddy, although he hadn't called her back yet. She had agreed to be the chair of the foundation, but she was just getting used to the necessary process of approving funds and facilitating the donations to the identified causes.

Marie waited in the foyer as Megan walked down the marvelous grand staircase.

"You look wonderful, as usual," Marie said with a motherly smile as she adjusted Megan's clothing. "Just stay aware. I don't think Jonathan's intentions focus solely on the foundation."

Megan chuckled. "You sound like the mom I never had."

The pair turned when they heard a knock on the front door. Megan gave Marie a quick hug. "I'll be home as soon as I can. If you wouldn't mind, please put on a pot of coffee for me for when I get back. I'm waiting for some information to do research tonight and I think I'll be up late."

"For the foundation?" Marie asked with a frown.

Megan looked down. "No, it would be for Nick."

Marie raised her eyebrows. "I hope you're not getting involved where you shouldn't be."

"It's just research, Marie, but thanks for being concerned. Please have the coffee ready."

"Okay, go have a great time. You should go out more. I know these past couple months have been difficult with Nick's recovery."

Megan smiled and gave Marie a quick hug before she opened the front door.

"Megan, you look lovely, as usual." Jonathan bent forward to give her a kiss on the cheek. He wore an expensive suit, and his cologne was pleasant.

"Hi Jonathan, you look great yourself." Megan smiled.

"We better be off then," Jonathan said as he offered her his arm.

As Megan pulled the front door closed behind her, she couldn't help but smile when she saw Marie roll her eyes.

"Have you been to the Blue Whale yet?" Jonathan asked as he helped Megan into the passenger side of the car. Megan was surprised she was being helped into a brand-new red Ferrari.

Megan waited until he had walked around the car, positioned himself in the driver's seat and buckled his seat belt. "No, I haven't heard much about it to be honest, but we usually don't frequent the restaurants in the summer. It gets a bit crowded with everyone flocking to the beach."

"That's true," Jonathan agreed.

"Is this new?" Megan asked as she looked around the car.

"Do you like it? I've never driven a Ferrari before. I'm renting it for awhile to see if I like how it drives."

"It's beautiful, but with the stop and go of the summer traffic and constant sea spray, I'd be afraid to own one near the beach."

"Funny you say that. It's very frustrating to drive a fast car that's stuck in traffic most of the time, but I needed something for now."

"I can see it as a topic of discussion for a lot of people near the boardwalk, but I'd be afraid to leave it alone while I was on the beach. Of course, the guys from the breakfast club would be eager to keep an eye on it for you."

"Is that the group of retired gentlemen hanging around the coffee shop across from the boardwalk every morning?"

"You know them," Megan said. "There's a lot to be discussed." She ticked off her fingers as she spoke. "The weather, fishing, crowds, cars, motorcycles, town business, politics."

Jonathan laughed as he listened. "Some things never change."

"Speaking of change, how long have you actually been back from London?"

Jonathan looked at her as he stopped the car for a red light. "To be honest, I just arrived yesterday morning. I'm glad we didn't go to dinner yesterday because I've still got some jet lag."

Megan didn't know how to respond. She was a bit unsettled that one of the first things Jonathan would do would be to race over to Misty Manor after landing in America. "I can't stay out late tonight. I have some research to do but I wanted to speak with you about the foundation and a recent visit we had with Pastor Lee at the shelter."

Jonathan arrived at the restaurant where an eager car valet ran to the car. Another opened Megan's door and helped her out. Jonathan slid out of the driver's side and handed the key fob to the valet. He hadn't used the car long enough to know if there was a valet mode. "Kit gloves and make sure there are no scratches when I get out."

"Of course, of course," the excited kid said as he got into the car.

When Jonathan reached Megan she said, "that's the next reason I wouldn't use an expensive car near the beach."

Jonathan looked back over his shoulder. "Thankfully, it's fully insured."

He placed his hand on the small of Megan's back and guided her to the front door of the restaurant. He gave his name at the hostess stand and they were asked to wait while she notified the waitstaff they had arrived. They were escorted to a lovely table placed in front of a cathedral window, which afforded a view of the ocean. The linen tablecloth was blue and matched perfectly with the posh decorative design.

"This is beautiful," Megan said as her chair was pulled out for her.

"I've heard some great things about this restaurant," Jonathan said as he sat and smiled at her.

"It looks lovely." Megan smiled to herself as she couldn't help comparing having dinner at a luxurious restaurant with enjoying the best boardwalk hot dog with Nick.

As they waited to be advised of the menu, Megan turned to Jonathan. "Why did you decide to leave London and return to America?"

Jonathan looked her in the eyes, took her hand and said, "That's one of the things I wanted to speak to you about. Perhaps after dinner would be best."

❦

46

Nick pushed the wooden door of the men's restroom open and spoke loudly. "This is officer Nick Taylor. Is anyone in here?"

Hearing nothing but silence he looked back toward the detective.

"This is Detective Wilson from the State Park Police. Is anyone in here? We are coming in to search the premises. Speak out if anyone is here."

Wilson then nodded toward Nick and pointed to the right. Both men slowly walked through the bathroom, carefully checking the floor for anyone's shoes, and opening the wooden bathroom stalls doors. They also checked the back room where the showers were located and once again found the bathroom to be completely empty.

"Damn," Wilson said. "Let's go round everyone up and see if anyone has any information. If not, I'll start a search tonight including the dogs."

As they were exiting the bathroom, Bob Flowers walked in and registered surprise to see the two men together inside. He raised his eyebrows. "Group effort?"

Wilson scowled as he looked at Flowers. "Have you seen Mr. Dante Valentino?"

"I don't know," Flowers said. "He was with us earlier."

"What about after you all stormed out of the cabin?"

"Excuse me?"

"Amber informed us that you were part of the revolt."

"It wasn't a revolt, but I believe we weren't to be held as prisoners. If we must stay at this mud hole another day, we're entitled to get a little fresh air."

Wilson nodded as he held his hat. "Yes, that's true, but unfortunately another one of you is missing."

"Then why the hell aren't you out there looking for him instead of sneaking around the bathroom?"

Wilson tapped Nick on the arm. "That's exactly what we plan on doing. Thank you, Mr. Flowers. Once you're done here, do not leave the camp. Either stay in the general common area or return to the cabin or mess hall when dinner is served."

Flowers gave a mock salute. "Yes, sir. Permission to pee, sir?"

Wilson disgustedly shook his head as the two officers left the bathroom.

"I'll go back and take another look in the cabin in case he returned," Nick said as he pointed in that direction.

"Good, because I'm going to the parking lot to call in reinforcements. I'm not waiting around on this one. I'll tell them to get the search and rescue dogs ready. Meet me by the bonfire in ten minutes."

"Will do," Nick said with a nod.

As Wilson walked away, he looked back and said, "But if you happen to find this guy, walk toward the parking lot and give me a wave."

47

M egan and Jonathan listened as the waiter outlined the entree offerings for the evening. The restaurant served several eclectic meals which were all exquisite. There were no menus or prices. If a customer needed to know the price of the food or wine, they obviously couldn't afford to eat there. Jonathan chose a five-course meal for both which started with a cucumber gazpacho soup followed by a salad of baby arugula and goat cheese. Next was a lobster Bolognese dish. Their main entrée was a Beef Wellington followed by a French chocolate mousse. A sommelier had suggested a wine which would pair perfectly with dinner and then another berry wine for dessert. All followed by a dark rich roasted coffee for Megan and tea for Jonathan.

"I haven't eaten like this in a long while," Megan said as she tasted her food. "Marie is an excellent cook, but we like to keep it somewhat simple."

"I couldn't eat like this all the time," Jonathan said. "It's nice to have a taste of elegance on occasion. When was the last time you had Beef Wellington?"

Megan shook her head. "I honestly couldn't tell you."

"We had it quite often in London. It's a steak dish of English origin. Basically, it's a fillet steak coated with foie gras pate and duxelles, then wrapped in pastry and baked."

Megan smiled to herself, knowing the last time she made a meat dish wrapped in pastry, she had to slam the tube on the counter to release the dough. "It tastes heavenly, Jonathan."

"I'm glad you like it," he said with a small smile as he looked at Megan. "When you've finished, why don't you tell me about the shelter in Misty Point?"

Megan took a sip of her coffee and placed her delicate China cup back on the saucer. She proceeded to explain to Jonathan who Pastor Lee was, as well as the attachment between his church and the shelter. She explained how the food pantry had started and expanded to help those in need without a place to stay.

"Sounds like quite a place."

"It is," Megan said. "There are many young people who flock to the beach in the summer looking for housing. The police department is happy to work in conjunction with the shelter to make sure the shelter and beach stay safe and clean. The hospital sends over a social worker to help with long term plans."

Jonathan nodded. "Sounds very organized as well."

"He does a great job," Megan agreed. "Which is why we would like to help support him. I know my grandmother didn't always believe in throwing cash at certain situations, so we have some specific suggestions. We'd like to offer an emergency cash reserve, but also plan to have food delivered when needed as well as supply bedding, clothes, and hygiene products. We can keep them stocked to fifty people and restock as necessary. The foundation will take care of the cost."

"That sounds generous," Jonathan said as he sipped his tea.

"The only problem is I don't know how Teddy normally sets this up so I need you to explain what I want, and we can fine tune the details later. I've asked Pastor Lee to send a list of his needs in writing so we can present everything at the next board meeting."

"Done." Jonathan smiled as he looked at Megan. "I'll bring the concept up immediately and, as you said, we'll hammer the details when we have the request in writing."

Megan finished her coffee and placed her cup on her saucer. "Thank you, Jonathan. The meal was delicious, and I appreciate the opportunity to discuss this charity with you."

Jonathan nodded as he finished his tea. "It's still early enough for us to take a ride and talk a bit." He then turned and gestured to the waiter for their bill.

48

Ten minutes later, Nick stood in the clearing and watched Wilson scowl as he headed back to the camp.

Wilson looked at Nick. "Find him?"

Nick shook his head. "Nope, I've gathered everyone in the cabin, and we can all go to the mess hall for dinner in a few minutes, but no Dante Valentino to be found."

"Damn. We've got to find him. The question is whether he's a runner or has met some harm of his own."

"What about reinforcements?" Nick asked as he looked around.

"Officers are being called in and they're bringing the dogs. We're finding this guy one way or another."

The men walked into the cabin and saw the group in the common area. Bob Flowers was changing his T-shirt and shot them a dirty look. Alberto was sitting on the couch, staring out the window, but looked up immediately. Veronica was combing her hair and trying to apply makeup using a hand mirror from her glamour bag while Nancy sat in her bunk reading a Stephen King novel. Amber stood nervously in the corner.

Wilson held his arms up to the group. "I know these questions will seem redundant but when was the last time anyone saw Dante Valentino?"

The group looked at each other and shrugged.

"The last time we saw him, he walked out with you," Nancy Rogan replied. "You pulled him out to question him and I know I didn't see him again."

"That's not true," Nick said. "He was in this cabin while we were waiting for Amber."

"And he was with all of you when you stormed out of here," Amber added.

"Has anyone seen him since then?" Wilson asked again.

They all agreed he was not seen after leaving the cabin.

Nick looked toward Wilson. He alone knew what was said in the interview, but Wilson was closed mouthed.

They all heard a bell ring in the distance. Amber moved forward. "I believe that means dinner is ready. Is it okay if we go to the mess hall?"

"You're not prisoners, but be aware, there will be a lot of officers arriving in the next thirty minutes so try to keep it to the mess hall, bathroom, bonfire or cabin." Wilson then gestured out the door.

Amber stayed behind as the others made their way over to dinner. "You know what Nancy Rogan said isn't true." Amber watched them from the porch, making sure they didn't hear what she was telling Wilson and Nick. "We were all in the cabin together. Nick, you were watching them until I got back from my interview with Detective Wilson and then you both left to discuss something. That's when they all got agitated and walked out."

Nick nodded as he looked at Wilson. "That's exactly right. Dante was in the cabin, and I made sure he remembered that you wanted to see his phone."

"I don't know what's going on here, but we're going to find out," Wilson said as he crossed his arms over his uniform. "Amber, you go into the mess hall and continue to keep an eye on them. Listen to what they're saying. I'm sure you'll hear plenty of complaints but keep track of anything important that's said about Dante's plans or comments. Also, let me know where your boss is. He was here and now he's gone again. Let me know if he's in there helping Phil make the food or something."

Nick nodded as he listened to the plan. He then tapped on Wilson's arm. "Before we leave, I want to search his stuff. I think he was fussing around in his backpack. I want to see what he may have taken with him." Nick turned to Amber. "Keep an eye out by the door for us?"

"Good idea," Wilson agreed as they made their way to the bunk. The bed was messed with blankets bunched up in a corner.

Nick checked under the pillow and under the bunk. He pulled out a backpack and opened it up. One by one he lifted items out of the backpack. "His wallet and phone are gone, but it looks like his toiletries and clothes are still here. Plenty of condoms, a magazine, and headphones."

"All replaceable if he didn't want to attract attention," Wilson said. "He wouldn't have left with a backpack, if he was planning on making a run for it."

"None of this is very helpful."

"Nick, come with me to the parking lot to meet the other officers. They should be arriving any moment."

"You got it," Nick said. "I'm going to make a quick pit stop first. I'll walk Amber over to the mess hall."

Wilson gave a curt nod and walked off.

"Nick, what's going on?" Amber grabbed his arm as she spoke. "Another person is missing. I'm getting scared. Isn't there a way for all of us to leave?"

"I have no idea what's happening, but this whole retreat has been very strange. Where the hell is Daman? He was just yelling at you, and he's gone again."

Amber shrugged. "He keeps saying how he's going to lose everything once word of the retreat and the death gets out. I think he keeps calling his lawyers or something."

"How is he getting in and out of the park then without being seen by the officers?" Nick asked. "Hiking through the woods?"

"I have no idea, but that's what he said. Speaking of hiking, how are you holding up? You were supposed to be here on an easy assignment. I don't think you've slept in two days. How is your leg and when was the last time you ate? Megan's going to kill me for not watching out for you."

Nick gave a low groan. "Don't point it out or I'll crash. I'm running on adrenaline right now. You're right. I'm going to need to take a nap, get a hot shower, and a meal soon. If not, I'm going to crash big time."

"Then you'll be set back another three months in your recovery. Nick, step back and let Wilson and the State Park Police do their job. You were sent here to serve as security for the camp."

"And look how well that turned out," Nick said. "Not one damn thing has gone right with this whole retreat."

"For either one of us. Megan's always trying to get me to work full time for the Stanford Foundation, so this may be the time to take the plunge. I'm not going to have a job after this fiasco."

"That may be the case for both of us," Nick said as he stopped walking. "Let me stop at the bathroom and go meet Wilson. Keep an eye out and let us know of anything important."

"You got it," Amber said as she reached over and gave him a quick hug.

49

Megan turned her face toward the breeze as the Ferrari sped down the roadway. "I hope there's no cop taking radar on this road."

"I don't know about now, but there never used to be." Jonathan was speeding on an empty road, near one of the marshes, on the outskirts of town. "I wanted to see what she could do before I make a decision."

Megan nodded as she watched the marsh speed by. "Like I said, it's a beautiful car, but probably not very practical if you're living in a beach town. So, what are your plans?"

Jonathan turned off the quiet road and headed toward the ocean. Megan could see the boardwalk lights in the distance. Normally, she'd be able to see the Ferris wheel and other amusements. The attractions were only open on the weekends in October. In another few weeks, they would be closed for the season. Megan looked forward to the holidays but felt sad when the town shut down until spring.

"Let's take a walk on the boardwalk. We should be able to get coffee or tea and talk," Jonathan said as he cruised toward the ocean.

After a few minutes, they found a parking spot with easy access to the boardwalk. They disembarked and walked up the ramp. Megan loved being near the beach at night. Regardless of the month, the sound of the ocean, reflection of moonlight, and the smell of salt spray, held a special allure.

They walked toward a bench and sat down. Megan was very aware when Jonathan grabbed her hand along the way.

"What's wrong?" Megan asked as she looked at him.

He looked down at his hands. "Nothing is wrong. It's just that I must make some decisions and I wanted some input from you."

"What kind of decisions?"

"About my career and I'm worried about Teddy."

"I've tried to call him several times in the last two days, and I haven't been able to reach him."

"That's part of the reason I finalized my affairs in London. I don't think he's feeling well but he's not telling me what's going on. I wondered if he said anything to you."

"Nothing at all." Megan shook her head.

"I know he's been getting medical testing, because I've seen some of the notices in the mail. He's very closed mouthed about all of this." Jonathan shrugged. "I don't know what he's being tested for or how it will impact everything."

"Have you asked him point blank?"

"He hasn't been home since yesterday. I think he may be in a facility. There was a message on our voice mail confirming his appointment, but not the location."

"I hope he's okay," Megan said realizing how much of the operation depended solely on Teddy. It was something she determined to fix immediately. She loved Teddy but didn't want to see her grandmother's hard work compromised in any way.

"I'll speak to him directly when he's back. His health will help determine how I set myself up here in America. I'm not sure if I'll assume his practice or go in another direction." Jonathan turned to look at Megan. "Some of that decision also depends on you."

"What do you mean?"

Jonathan sighed and looked off toward the ocean. "If my father retires, I wouldn't expect you to automatically accept me as the new legal representative. I'm aware that you aren't familiar with my style as an attorney and know I've worked mainly in Europe."

"I'm beginning to think we should have a succession planning meeting with Teddy. I don't want to see the Stanford Foundation compromised in any way. There's a lot of money involved, and I want to make sure it's all protected. Teddy has a greater working knowledge than I do. I've learned a lot this past year but now feel I need to learn the lion's share regarding the company. Some of that information would affect how things move forward."

"I agree, that's a good idea."

Jonathan turned to Megan and took her hand. "I know you're seeing Nick and I know he's healing. What I don't know is how solid that relationship is, and I won't ask, but I do want you to know, if Nick is no longer in the picture, for any reason, I'm there for you. I'd like the chance to be closer, but I'll respect your current situation."

Megan was speechless at Jonathan's sentiment. She never had to worry about a line of suitors in her life. Nick's reluctance to further their relationship was based on his pride and health. Although he didn't know she was worth a quarter billion dollars, he knew she had more money than him. If anything happened to Nick, she would question the motives of anyone else who was interested. Jonathan may have a better idea of what her true worth was, so she already had trust issues.

"I don't know what to say, Jonathan," Megan said. "I can't even think right now. Nick and I are taking it one step at a time. We want to wait until he heals, and my grandmother's estate is completely settled."

"I understand and I'm not asking for any commitment or promises. I wanted you to know how I feel. I can wait for you if I must."

Megan nodded. "Thank you, I appreciate your honesty." After a few awkward moments, Megan took a deep breath. "I think we should call it a night. You need to go check on your father and I have some research to do."

Jonathan squeezed her hand. "I agree. I still have jet lag." He looked at his watch. "Right now, it's 1:00 a.m. in London."

"You need time to adjust and get some proper sleep before making any decisions."

"I know," Jonathan said as he smiled and kissed her on the cheek. He then stood and pulled her up with him. "Let's go. I'll take you home."

Megan felt relieved as they walked down the ramp and got into the red Ferrari. Everything had been a little too fast for her tonight. More than ever, she missed her quiet summer with Nick.

50

Nick reached the parking lot and watched Detective Wilson direct his officers.

"I want two officers to follow Trail A, two on Trail B and two on Trail C. Look for our missing man and any signs that he passed through. We don't know if he decided to take off, was involved in the first murder or ran into trouble himself." The officers asked a few questions and then scattered to search as much as they could before dark.

Wilson turned to Nick. "I'm assuming you didn't find Dante or anything else we can use."

"Nothing, but I'm going to search the woods where I found Dante and Veronica having a tryst yesterday."

"That's interesting," Wilson mused. "Those two hooked-up without knowing each other."

Nick shrugged. "We're led to believe. I've seen it happen that way. People that aren't settled, acting out. We've got a shelter in town that had a similar problem last summer. Anyway, I'm going to check it out. I'll be back in ten minutes and let you know."

"Okay, I'll be here waiting for the search and rescue dog team.

They should be here any minute. We're going to need an item of Dante's. Preferably, something he recently wore."

Nick nodded. "I believe there were a few things in his backpack. If I don't find anything in the woods, I'll run up to the cabin, grab something and bring it back."

"Good, go," Wilson said as he gestured toward the path.

Nick turned and walked up the path. His leg was tingling, and he was getting tired. He hoped they found something soon or he'd have to beg off for a while to rest. If that happened, the best he could hope for was desk duty for another three months before Davis let him in the field. He'd be happy to beg for the beach patrol just so he could be out and about again, but that wouldn't be needed until the town started prepping for the spring weather.

Nick found the entrance to the path near one of the clearings by the cabin. He separated the brush and slowly walked forward. It was dark in areas that weren't penetrated by the fading sunlight. He scanned back and forth looking for anything that may indicate Dante was recently there, but he didn't see any pieces of clothing or broken branches.

When he reached the center, he made a slow circle, but didn't find anything suspicious.

Nick left the clearing, retraced the path, and headed to the cabin. No one was about so he assumed they were all in the mess hall eating or complaining. Hopefully, Amber would bring them a clue to follow.

He reached the steps, went into the cabin and up to Dante's bunk. Rummaging through the backpack, he spotted a rolled up dirty T-shirt. Picking it up by a tiny corner of the sleeve he put it inside Dante's pillowcase and carried it outside with him.

51

Megan thanked Jonathan as he opened the door to the Ferrari. They left the boardwalk and drove straight to Misty Manor.

"Let me walk you to the door," Jonathan said. "If anything happens to you, Nick will have my head when he gets back."

Megan let out a small chuckle. "That may be true. Hopefully, everything is calm at the house tonight."

The couple walked up the steps. "Open the door and make sure all is well before I leave, please."

Megan did what he asked. She unlocked and opened the door. As she greeted the dogs, she turned off the alarm and let the dogs run outside. "Everything looks okay," Megan said to Jonathan as they stood on the porch.

"Great. I'll be off then. Think about what I said tonight. I need to find out what my father is up to and make a few decisions about a career here in America. Some of the future is dependent on decisions you make, whether it's in the romance or business department, and I'm asking for nothing other than being honest with me."

Megan nodded. "I understand and as soon as I talk with Teddy and we meet about a few things, I'll have some answers. As far as

Nick is concerned, we're together as a couple. We have a history as far back as high school. He's recovering and I'm not ready to change anything in my life right now concerning our relationship."

Jonathan nodded and leaned forward to give her a kiss on the cheek. "Goodnight, Megan. Thank you for a wonderful dinner. I needed a fun night out to clear my head."

"Goodnight, Jonathan," Megan said as she watched him walk off toward the driveway. She understood the turmoil that accompanied change but the only way to work through it was to keep going. Certainly, his path would open for him soon.

Megan turned her attention toward the beach. She looked over the sand, which was now bathed in moonlight. Next, she turned toward the waves. "Dudley? Bella?" *Where did those dogs get off to?* Normally they frolicked on the beach right in front of the house, but she didn't see them. She walked off the porch and down to the sand. She didn't hear any commotion that would lead her to believe they chased something or someone. She had been so attuned to Jonathan's somber mood, she admitted to herself, she may not have been paying attention the way she should have.

Megan reached the sand and looked right and left as she walked toward the water. She called their names and began to feel alarmed. This was not like the dogs at all. Reaching the water's edge, she listened for any splashing or noise that would indicate where they were, but she only heard the soft crest of the waves on the beach.

"Dudley? Bella?" Megan called out but was afraid her call was quickly lost in the wind as it whipped in from the water. She turned to walk back to the house and as she neared the edge of the beach, she heard a noise to her right. She called the dogs once again and was rewarded when they came crashing through the beach scrub and ran toward her, tongues hanging out. "Where were you boys? You had me scared to death." The dogs ran up to the porch and waited for Megan to reach the top step. Jumping on her, they let her know how happy they were that she was finally home. She bent down to pet them and scratch their heads.

"Where did you go?" Megan asked as she cuddled Dudley's head against her. As she did so, she felt something strange near his neck. When she looked, she found a piece of paper wound around his collar several times. Carefully, she pulled it from his collar and smoothed it open. "Damn, Luther." There was a list of names and she realized it was sent by Luther or one of his team via the dog. Realizing her vulnerability made her more nervous. She swallowed and read the list.

NORTH MARSH STATE Park

1. Bob Flowers – Antacus Pharmaceuticals
2. Veronica Lane – Antacus Pharmaceuticals
3. Alberto Ortiz – Antacus Pharmaceuticals
4. Felix Cooper – Salacia Medical Supply
5. Dante Valentino – LPW Medical Records
6. Nancy Rogan – LPW Medical Records
7. Joe Daman – Portal Healthcare Company CEO
8. Phil Beckman – Camp Manager hired through Portal
9. Amber Montgomery – Portal Healthcare Company
10. Nick Taylor – Misty Point Police Department
11. Detective Wilson – NJ State Park Police
12. Public – outsiders?

52

Nick met Wilson in the parking lot and handed him the pillowcase. Inside was the dirty T-shirt. "Here, I tried not to touch the shirt to confuse the scent. As you can guess, I went to one clearing and checked out as much as I could. It was almost completely dark, but I didn't stumble across anything or anyone in the clearing."

"Thanks," Wilson said as he took the pillowcase, opened it, and looked at the shirt. "None of the officers have reported back so I can only assume they haven't found anyone either."

As they spoke, a black SUV drove up. An officer popped out of the driver's side and came around and opened the back door. Two bloodhounds jumped out of the car. They immediately looked at their handler and came to attention.

Officer Field walked over to Wilson and nodded. "Good evening. What's going on?"

Wilson reached out and shook his hand. "Thanks for coming over, Frank. We have a missing executive who was on retreat here. Six executives arrived yesterday, and one was murdered yesterday afternoon. Today, another has gone missing. We don't know if he absconded or if he's in trouble. I didn't want to wait to start searching.

Some of the officers are on the trails but I haven't heard back from anyone."

"That's fine. The dogs do better at night anyway. Less interfering smells from cookouts and people milling about. You got something for them with a scent?" Frank Field nodded toward the pillowcase.

"Yes, there's a dirty T-shirt belonging to our missing man in here."

"That should be good enough," Frank said. "I bought Sadie and Millie with me tonight. Sadie was trained as an air-scenter so when we let her go, she'll smell the officers, and probably yesterday's cadaver but she'll smell the missing executive as well. If she finds something she'll start barking. Millie is a tracker, so I'll keep her on lead but once she gets a sniff of the shirt, she'll track the exact route our guy took on his way out. They're both good for a couple hours and should be able to smell someone up to a couple miles away. Millie and I will start at the place your executive was last seen so when you're ready, you can show me where that is."

"Will do," Nick said. "There's a small chance of rain. Is that problem?

"Are you kidding me? This weather is great for the dogs. You'd be amazed at what they can do and in what conditions. Honestly, evening is the best for them. The scent is stronger, sound carries further and they're fine in the brush. Their eyesight is much keener than ours as well. The officers are more at risk at night from an unseen hazard, if not from tripping over a downed tree branch."

As they ended their discussion, two of the officers returned from the path that led to the ocean. Wilson met them with a question. "See or hear anything we need to know about?" Officer Cheryl Mead shook her head. "Nothing except a few kids on the beach smoking pot. I don't think he went that way. It got dark while we searched so we can't be completely sure of anything, but it just didn't feel right."

Officer Field nodded. "Okay, please show me the place he was last seen."

Nick led the group back to the cabin. "All of the executives were in the cabin together. They got into a huff since the investigation kept their activity limited and walked out. We have no idea which way he went."

"Okay, I'll let Sadie go free and we'll track Dante's steps with Millie. Can I have that pillowcase please?" Wilson handed over the pillowcase. Frank Field opened it and looked inside. He then held the case open and down to the noses of the two dogs. Both sniffed the inside of the case for a few seconds and started to get excited. Within a few seconds, Frank let Sadie off her lead, and she bounded into the woods. "And we're off." He turned to Wilson and Nick. "We should have a trail soon. You're welcome to follow behind Millie and me but stay about ten feet back."

Both nodded their understanding. Field gave a command to Millie, and they started walking toward the bathrooms. Millie pulled Frank as she sniffed the ground and went toward the bathroom. She sniffed the doors and the ground and then doubled back and headed to the back of the cabin. She found a hidden trail and started to lead in that direction. The men watched Millie at work and were amazed at the precision of twists and turns she took. About ten minutes into the wood, they all heard Sadie barking in the distance.

Frank turned to Wilson and Nick. "They both seem to be converging on the same area so that's a pretty good sign we'll find your man. I don't know what condition he's in. Sadie sounds like she's not moving. If your guy was on the run, her barking would be moving as well."

Wilson and Nick looked at each other, prepared for what they might find. Millie's path met up with Sadie in another five minutes. Frank Field called off the dogs and gave them a treat while Nick and Wilson pulled out a flashlight torch and searched for Dante. After a minute, Frank nodded to where Sadie was barking. "Not sure, but I think I see a foot sticking out from behind that rock."

When they searched between a large rock and fallen tree, they found Dante's body. Wilson pulled a pair of gloves out of his pocket, immediately knelt, and felt for a pulse. He had to roll the body and eventually Wilson stood and shook his head. "He's gone. I can't see enough of the body to know exactly what happened but he's cold.

From what I felt, I think rigor mortis has started to set so he's been this way a couple of hours, at least." Wilson turned to Nick. "What time did you last see him?"

"I was in the cabin with all of them when you returned with Amber, and you and I left together. That was after lunch, but we were only gone for thirty minutes before Amber came to find us and let us know they had all walked out."

"Timing sounds about right then." Wilson stood up. "We don't know if it's murder or something else, but I've got to get a team in here as well as the ME. I'm going to radio in as much as I can. We'll need lights." He looked at Officer Field. "C'mon, Frank. Let's go back to the camp." Wilson turned toward Nick. "Do you mind staying here and keeping watch? I don't want anything or anybody coming near that body or the crime scene until the ME arrives."

"No, I'm fine."

Wilson handed him a pair of nitrile gloves. "Try not to touch anything or contaminate the scene. I don't smell anything funny, so I doubt it was a toxin." He looked around for a moment before turning to Frank. "If there was anyone else out here, the dogs would know, right?"

Frank nodded. "Yes, they're not sensing anyone else, or Sadie would be barking or running."

Wilson nodded. "Okay, I think all is safe. Just watch the area and make sure it stays as pure as possible until we can start logging everything. I want to put an officer on the rest of the executives as well. Something is very wrong here."

"You got it," Nick said as took the gloves. "I've had plenty of training with dead bodies and Chen as well, so I know what he'll expect. You'd better go and get the party started."

Wilson nodded, touched Frank Fields on the arm and they started back toward the camp. The dogs were still excited and led the way without need of light or scent.

53

Megan closed the door to the foyer and made sure everything was locked. She turned on the alarm and leaned against the door. She jumped when she heard Marie's voice from the kitchen door. "How did it go?"

"As expected," Megan said as she shrugged. "Jonathan's moved back from London and is trying to find his new normal. A lot will depend on Teddy's health and my decision as to whether he'll be the successor to Teddy as the estate attorney. He's a bit lost right now." Megan walked toward the foyer as she spoke to Marie and purposefully did not tell her of Jonathan's romantic interests. He needed to find himself before he chose a partner and Megan was already dedicated to Nick.

"The coffee is hot, rich and dark, as requested," Marie said as they sat at the kitchen table. "Did you have dessert?"

"Oh yes," Megan said. "I'll have to go running with Georgie for the next week to work off that meal."

"Was it tasty? I've heard about the restaurant but haven't heard anyone talk about reviews."

"I can tell you the food, all courses, were simply delicious. The atmosphere was gorgeous."

Marie frowned for a second before Megan continued. "Marie, the issue is we live down the shore and near the beach. The place is too fancy for people visiting the beach and the people who live here year-round probably couldn't afford it. As a matter of fact, I wonder who owns that restaurant. I'll have to investigate that."

"And who paid for dinner tonight?"

"Jonathan paid," Megan said as she looked at Marie with a questioning glance.

"Are you sure he's not charging it back to the foundation as a business meal?"

Megan paused for a moment. "I have no idea, Marie. He didn't mention anything of the sort."

"I know it's none of my business but that's where you need to get more involved in the financial administration of the foundation. Your grandmother was fastidious about that. Every expenditure had to be approved by her. She wanted everything detailed which also helped with audits and such. I only know because she asked me to help her with her paperwork at times."

Megan nodded. "You're absolutely right. I've been worried about the donation process, but I haven't paid much attention to administration finances. I'll have to take the reins very soon. Tonight, however, I want to see if I can help Nick by getting some research done."

"I don't know exactly what you're doing, which is fine by me, but I have a large thermos filled with that same coffee and I placed a tray of snacks in the library as well."

"Thank you, Marie. It's very much appreciated."

"I assume you're setting up shop in the library?"

Megan nodded. "Yes, I know grandmother used the small office off the foyer, but as you noticed, I recently set up my computer at the cherrywood desk in the library. I used to be a great investigative journalist and I'd like to get back to it in some way if I can. Helping Nick with information would be a great way to restart."

"I'm glad to hear that. You're finally coming around and making

Misty Manor and the Stanford Foundation your own. Your grand-mother would be so proud."

Megan went over to Marie and gave her a big hug about the shoulders. "Thanks, Marie. I'll see you in the morning."

"I'll be in the kitchen, but I'll wait till you come in before I start cooking. Lord knows how late you'll be up tonight."

Smiling, Megan picked up her coffee cup and walked out of the kitchen.

54

N ick stood in the dark and listened. He heard a gentle breeze blowing through the trees as well as a small rustle of leaves. Thankfully it was warm, even though it was October. His leg was beginning to bother him, so he used his torch to find a place to rest. He didn't want to go anywhere near the rock or fallen tree associated with the crime scene. Resting against another rock across the path, he relaxed until he heard an owl whistle. Nick knew from his past training that in addition to hoots, owls could screech, shriek, chirp, and whistle. Owl sounds are loud and low in pitch so the sound can travel easily through the night sky. But that specific owl whistle was one he would always recognize from his limited past training.

He immediately stood up and looked around.

"What's going on?"

Nick jumped at the quiet voice in his ear even though he was expecting it. "Damn it, Luther. You've got to stop sneaking up on me."

Luther quietly chuckled. "Seriously, what the hell is going on around here?"

"I don't know. You can see there's another man down. I'm playing guard until Wilson gets back here with Chen and the crime scene techs. How long have you been here?"

"Not too long. I made sure Megan got home safely and sent the list of names to her to research."

"Got home? Where was she?" Nick asked.

Luther was quiet for a few seconds before he answered. "It appears she had a meeting about the homeless shelter and a donation she wants to make."

Nick nodded in the dark. "She was talking about Pastor Lee. Maybe I'm nuts letting her do this research. Captain Davis would kill me if he knew she was even aware of what's going on."

"To that point, does Davis know what's going on?"

"He doesn't know about any of this," Nick whispered to the dark.

"Then don't worry about it right now. I hear she was very good at her old job, so let her work it. The more information you have, the better."

"That's true and at this point, we clearly need something," Nick said. "I don't want her getting involved in any other way."

"My team and I have been circulating the perimeter. No one saw this happen, but we also haven't seen anyone in and out of the park except for the arrogant CEO, but I think he's more bluster than anything else. For what it's worth, I'm pretty sure you're dealing with an insider for this. Megan's research is exactly what you need. I'll check on her in the morning and we'll make sure you get the information one way or another."

"Thanks, just keep her out of this and safe," Nick said as he rested on the rock.

"Hey, you told me to keep an eye on her and she asked me to keep an eye on you and you're both damn lucky I don't have anything else going on right now." Luther stopped midsentence. "I hear a dog. They're probably on their way. I'm gone. Talk to you later."

"Hey, how come the dogs didn't smell you earlier?" Nick asked in the dark.

"We're used to using a certain oil on our skin to hide the human scent."

Nick didn't have a chance to respond before he heard barking. He couldn't see Luther but didn't feel his presence anymore, so Nick was sure he'd gone in time.

A few minutes later, he heard shouts. "Taylor? Everything okay here?" Nick flashed his torch up and down to guide them the rest of the way. Wilson was back with Officer Frank Field and one dog, the tracker, Millie.

Nick immediately stood. "Yes, nothing has happened or changed since you left."

"Millie's been barking up a storm here on her way back and Sadie was going crazy. Probably smelling everything now that it's nighttime."

"I imagine so," Nick said. "Thankfully, it appears to be a peaceful balmy night."

"Damn lucky for October," Wilson agreed.

"Did you get hold of Chen?" Nick asked.

"Yes, he's on his way with a CSI team. I've got officers bringing lights and other equipment."

"Good, Millie. Stand down," Field said as he rewarded the dog.

"What's going on back at the cabin?" Nick asked as they waited.

"I put a couple of officers on there as well. At this point, we need to secure whatever we can. It doesn't mean that one of the other executives did this, but I can't take the chance of another one leaving or becoming a victim. We don't know what the hell is going on, but we will soon."

As they were speaking, investigators arrived. It seemed mere seconds before lights were set up, crime scene tape cordoned off the scene, a logbook was started and techs in biohazard suits were photographing and cataloging the scene.

"You guys really have a problem with nighttime, don't you?" They looked up to see Dr. Victor Chen. "What have we got tonight?"

Wilson started talking first. "Another executive went missing several hours ago. This time, we got the dogs and didn't wait to search. Millie and Sadie found him quickly."

"When did you last see him alive?" Chen asked as he looked at the dead man.

"He was in the cabin with me and the other executives this afternoon," Nick said. "I left to speak to Wilson alone for a bit and they all took off. This one never returned."

"What's his name?"

"Dante Valentino. He was at the retreat on behalf of LPW Medical Records. Ever hear of that company, Doc?"

Chen shook his head. "I know they have software out there, but I haven't used any of their products." Chen examined the body. "Looks like rigor has set in. He's stiff and from the little I can see, he has lividity on his side, so he's been in this position a couple of hours, at least."

"That sounds about right to us when we tried to put together a timeline," Wilson agreed.

They watched as Chen pulled up Dante's shirt, retrieved a long thermometer from his bag and inserted it in the man's right upper abdomen. "We'll know the liver temperature in just a few minutes."

Nick tried to look away as Officer Field tapped Wilson on the arm. "You don't need us here anymore, so I'll bring Millie back to camp. We'll stay about 30 minutes in case something comes up but then I'll bring the dogs back home. You know how to reach me."

"Yes, thanks so much, Frank. I appreciate all your work. Without Sadie and Millie, we may not have found this guy for days."

"No problem. That's what they're trained for."

"They're invaluable," Wilson said. "Thanks again."

Nick nodded goodbye although Officer Field probably couldn't see him in the dark. He didn't want to watch Chen check his thermometer. He'd seen plenty of dead bodies in the field. They were found in various positions whether murdered or from natural death. He was used to gruesome expressions on their faces as well as blood splatter and all kind of body fluids at a scene. As a responding officer, he was happy when the crime scene techs showed up and he could walk away, or a sheet was pulled over the deceased. He couldn't stomach watching the team examine the body and never liked when he was sent to observe a particularly important autopsy to discover the cause of death.

"Any idea how he died?" Wilson asked. "We didn't stay near him long enough to determine if it was murder or suicide."

"Why would you think suicide?" Chen asked as he looked at Wilson.

"No reason unless somehow his death was linked to the last body. Sometimes you get a murder, suicide."

"Assuming they knew each other before the retreat, but they didn't work for the same company, right?"

"No," said Wilson shaking his head.

"This is a clear case of murder," Chen said as he directed his light down to the body. The field had been lit with the lights they brought in, but Chen's torch showed a clear line of bruising around the neck. "This is classic garroting. It's a ligature strangulation, but the question is with what? Did you see any wire or fishing line" Chen asked as he looked around the body.

"No, we couldn't see much because of the dark," Wilson said. "I put gloves on, and I only rolled him slightly to check for a pulse. The minute I saw he was stiff, I backed off. Didn't touch anything else."

"And I've been on the scene the whole time. No one or animal came near him after that, so whatever was there should still be there," Nick offered.

"Good, I won't be able to tell how it was done until I get him back to the morgue. I'll have the techs sweep up all the brush and bring that back to the morgue as well. Maybe we'll find something under his fingernails if he tried to grab whatever was used as the ligature. If we find it in the debris field, we may be able to get something from it."

Wilson shook his head. "I'm setting up a temporary command post in the state office. I'm going to have to question everyone again but if I don't find anything I'll have to let these people go. I can't hold them here much more."

Chen pulled the thermometer out of Dante's abdomen and checked the temperature. "The body temp is appropriate for a couple of hours and the night is temperate, although it's getting damp. He would have cooled off a lot faster if it was winter." He wiped off the thermometer and placed it in a bag then looked up and called out to a tech. "Make sure you place his hands in paper bags. I'm done here."

Chen stood and pulled the men a few yards away from the body as the crime scene techs prepared Dante for transport to the morgue.

Wilson stood with his hands on his hips. "So, what do you think?"

Chen pulled off his gloves. "Another murder for sure. I can't tell you right now if it's the same killer, but I'll see if I can find anything that connects the two together. Obviously, this killer got close enough to strangle this guy so it may be someone he recognized. Hard to sneak up on someone when you're in the woods unless he had ear buds on and didn't hear him, but I don't see any signs of earbuds and you're saying no one has touched the body."

"How about his phone. Did you see his phone?" Nick asked.

"No," Chen said as he shook his head. "I took a wallet out of his pocket, but no phone. No earbuds. No source of music. If his phone is under the leaves or in the brush, hopefully it will come in with the debris field. If not, then you and your men can come back and comb the area to your heart's content."

"Interesting," Wilson said as he watched the techs. "We still have hours before daylight. Once your men leave, I'm going to place an officer here to watch the scene until we can get back. Nick and I have been on the run all day. We both need some food and rest before we start again.

Nick nodded his agreement. He was tired, hungry, sweaty and his leg burned, but he wasn't backing down. He felt partially responsible for what happened, and he didn't want anyone hanging any of it on a partial disability. His career was not going down that route.

The woods were getting cool with a slight breeze. The animals that normally would have prowled were scared away by the activity and spotlights, yet Nick would not have wanted that watch for the night.

"Anything else useful come back from the first victim?" Wilson asked.

"Not really," Chen said. "The post didn't reveal anything new. Felix was healthy. His death was caused by head trauma from the rock. Fractured skull, brain bleed. Unconsciousness, if not death, would have been almost instantaneously. We didn't get anything from fingernails, no signs of struggle, so once again, I think he knew who his attacker was. I didn't find any kind of drug trace or toxin on his clothes or in his system. The rock seems to indicate it was not premeditated."

"Okay, thanks," Wilson said as he nodded.

"My guys will be done soon. I'll call you tomorrow afternoon if I get anything back by then."

"Thanks," Wilson said as he turned to Nick. "C'mon, let's get out of here and let them finish up. We'll make sure the cabin is peaceful and then call it a night."

"Amen to that," Nick said as they walked through the dark woods back to camp.

55

Megan looked at the list of names as she called up screen after screen of files. She had a large, yellow legal pad and a separate page for everyone on the list. Although it upset her to see Amber and Nick's names on the list, Luther was correct not to limit the research to the executives. The CEO and camp manager would be checked, as well as her friends, to make sure there was nothing personal involved.

Megan started with simple information gleaned from public records. She noted everything she could on paper and would draw conclusions later. At times, you could find a simple piece of information such as a birthday on social media, confirm the date and that would unlock a lot of additional information in another area.

From her days as an investigative reporter, Megan had learned other ways of collecting information. She would use whatever means she could if it would help Nick.

Pouring another cup of rich coffee, Megan rubbed her eyes. It was 1:00 a.m. and she realized she wasn't used to the all-nighters she had pulled in college and the early days of working at the newspaper in Detroit. Since the news company where she worked was mostly virtual, the job had to be done and posted as quickly as possible to grab the scoop and headline. One of her strengths back then was doggedly staying on the job until it was complete. Although she hadn't pulled an all-nighter in a long time, she knew she could go to bed as soon as the job was done. After working for a couple hours, she realized she missed the work as well as the thrill of the chase. Once this was all over, maybe she'd go back to investigative research in some way.

Flipping the page, she entered the next name into the database she was currently working in, found her spot and started taking notes.

56

Wilson and Nick arrived at the cabin. They walked in hoping everyone had settled down. The officer inside was told to keep them separated and let them sleep, if possible, but apparently everyone was still awake and agitated.

"Thank goodness, you're back," Amber said as she sidled up to Nick. "What's going on? I haven't seen you since you left with the dogs."

"Did they tell you about Dante?"

"Nothing specific but I'm not expecting to hear anything good with all the activity I see."

Wilson approached the common area. The four executives were either in their bunk or in the common area. Phil Beckman was near the fireplace stoking a gentle fire. Joe Daman was standing near the window with his arms crossed.

"It's about time you're here," Daman yelled. "It's 1:00 a.m. and I'm being held like a common criminal. I demand to leave."

Bob Flowers laughed from his bunk as he tossed a small ball up and down. "Apparently, what's good for the goose is unacceptable for the gander."

"Shut up," Daman yelled across the room at Bob. He turned to Detective Wilson. "You can't hold me here."

Wilson puffed up and crossed his arms. "I can hold anyone at the scene that I need to and for questioning until we've cleared the scene. So, sit down and shut it."

"I'll report you," Daman screamed.

"Go ahead and while you're at it, include the plan you submitted when you booked this place."

Daman shoved a chair which fell to its side as he walked to the other side of the room. Wilson shot him a dirty look and held his hands up. "Everyone, calm down. As you just heard, no one is going anywhere for a while. I'm not going to discuss details, but I will be speaking to each one of you individually again. It's late, so I suggest we all get some rest, and we'll start in the morning. Once I've talked with each of you, we'll let you go into the office and make a call to your family or boss to make arrangements to leave. Until then, you're to keep to yourselves, including any discussion." Wilson turned to Phil and Joe. "There are plenty of extra bunks. This cabin sleeps 18 so I suggest you choose one and rest. Our officers will be up all night to assist with any problems or to escort anyone in need to the bathroom. One at a time."

"Are you going to tell us what happened to Dante?" Veronica asked, her hands shaking.

"No, ma'am, I'm not."

"Is it okay if I keep the fire going for another hour or so?" Phil Beckman asked. "It helps me relax."

"As long as you don't leave or talk to anyone, I'm fine with that. Some of us will be up so it will be comforting. Thank you," Wilson said as he nodded toward Phil.

The rest of the group relaxed in their bunks with hopes of falling asleep soon.

"Phil and I saved you some food and coffee," Amber said as she pointed at tin trays of food on the table. A silver 30 cup coffee urn sat on the side with creamers and sugar. "Quite frankly, you two look like you're about to drop."

"Thank you," Nick said. "If I don't get something to eat, I just may." Nick and Wilson sat near the table and spent the next 15 minutes eating the cold dinner but washed it down with hot coffee. "Who ever thought camp food could taste so good?"

Nick felt sleepy near the end of his meal. He put the plates in the garbage and headed toward his bunk. He pulled out clean clothes and using the small toilet closet in the corner, changed, and laid down. Thankfully, there were other officers to keep watch and he fell asleep within minutes.

Wilson finished eating and sat in his chair watching the room. Joe Daman sulked at a window on the other side of the common room. Amber also changed and got into her bunk to relax. Phil maintained a small fire. After 30 minutes, Wilson had a small meeting with the two officers who would be keeping watch through the night. He delivered explicit instructions for them to observe and keep a record of any activity or comments. If anyone created a disturbance, they were to be arrested and sent to the station in a squad car. "I'm going to the office to start the paperwork. I'll probably sleep there once I'm done but if anything happens, you're to notify me immediately."

The officers nodded that they understood their assignment and Wilson left.

"This is bull," Daman said as he walked over to one of the chairs in the common area and sat to watch Phil tend the fire.

57

Megan stirred when a glint of sunlight appeared through the heavy library curtains. Noisy gulls were out and looking for food.

The stiffness in her neck prevented her from moving quickly. She had put her head down on the desk for a moment and must have fallen asleep despite all the coffee. Lifting her head and shoulders, she stretched her neck. As she rolled her head from side to side, she heard crunching and cracking as her body began to loosen up.

Megan had researched as much information as possible. She requested public information that would be delivered via email when released. Next, she took the time to collate all her results onto one sheet of paper. She planned to add any extra information when she received it later today and somehow have Luther get the results to Nick.

"Megan? Are you in here?" Marie popped into the library, a look of concern on her face. "Have you been in here all night?"

"Yes," she said sheepishly. "I finished what I could do several hours ago and must have fallen asleep at the desk." She stood and stretched her back as she continued to loosen up.

Marie walked over to the desk and retrieved the thermos which was empty. "I'll put on a pot of coffee right now and fix you up a nice breakfast. Maybe you can take a nap after you eat."

"Sounds great, Marie."

"Give me ten minutes."

Megan nodded and headed back to her desk to review the final summary of results. She had created a file and entered the summary before she fell asleep. She wondered whether it was customary to vet any guests before they attended these events or simply trust the HR department of the sending corporation. The results were interesting if not a bit scary.

Megan jumped when she heard a tap on the library window. She looked up to see Luther's face peering in at her. He beckoned her to open the window which she did. The ocean breeze was quite refreshing although she normally never opened the library windows as the salty air was not healthy for the antique books in the room.

"Luther, is it at all possible you could ring a doorbell like a normal person?"

He laughed. "No, I doubt it. Better this way. I don't like to be in social situations more than a few seconds."

"That's been pretty obvious," Megan scowled.

"I'm heading over to the state park. I was wondering if you have any information for Nick."

"Yes, I have some but not all of it has returned yet."

"Can you give me what you have and then I'll get the rest later?"

"Of course, give me a minute." Megan went to her computer and printed out the single sheet with the summary. Walking back to the window she handed it to Luther. He spent a moment scanning the sheet and then folded it away into an inside pocket of his light jacket.

"Is the park open?" Megan asked. "Maybe I should run over there with some clothes or food for Nick?"

"No, the park is still closed to the public." Luther shook his head to emphasize his words.

"Then how will you get that information to Nick?" Megan looked up at Luther's face and then shook her head. "Never mind, I don't think I want to know."

"Right answer," Luther said. "Go get some rest. The camp is getting heated so it's likely you'll hear from Nick today."

"Thank goodness," Megan said. Her next words were interrupted when Marie came into the room.

"You opened the window? Those windows haven't been opened in years." Marie walked over to look outside. When Megan quickly turned, she noticed Luther wasn't anywhere in sight.

"I know," Megan said. "I wanted some air, but I didn't feel like walking out to the front deck just yet."

Marie reached up to close the window. "I'll get that for you. Your breakfast and coffee are ready in the kitchen. Why don't you splash cold water on your face, eat a little something then go upstairs and rest for a while?"

"That sounds like the best offer I've had all week," Megan said as they turned and walked out of the library.

58

Nick opened his eyes and realized he was in his bunk. Without moving he surveyed the room. The two officers were in the common area, and it didn't look like anyone else had stirred yet. He slowly rolled out of his bunk and stood on the wooden floor. Nearing the officers, he spied Joe Daman in a bunk to one side of the room and Phil Beckman in a bunk on the other side of the room.

Nick beckoned the officer nearest the door out onto the porch. "How did everything go through the night? I know it's only been four to five hours, but did anything happen?"

The officer shook his head. "Nothing much. The CEO stayed up and stewed for a while but eventually took a bunk. I think he was trying to wait us out, but he doesn't know that we're used to the night shift."

"Did Detective Wilson ever come back to the cabin?"

"No, he probably fell asleep in the office."

"I'm going to check on him. Then I'll take a quick shower and be back to help with crowd control."

As they spoke, Phil Beckman walked out of the cabin and onto the porch. He stretched his arms overhead. "Permission to use the bathroom? Then maybe I can start making some coffee and breakfast for this happy crowd?"

The officer leaned into the cabin door and called to the other officer. "I'm going to walk Mr. Beckman to the bath and to the mess hall. You good with everyone else?" When he heard the other officer reply in the affirmative, he nodded to Phil that he would accompany him.

"I'd better go so I can be back to help. I know Wilson needs to take statements from everyone who was here yesterday." Nick stepped off the porch and headed to the bathroom and then the park office. He knocked on the office door and opened it to find Wilson slumped in the large office chair. Nick rushed over to Wilson and began to feel for a pulse in his neck.

"Get the hell off me," Wilson muttered. "What are you doing?"

Nick stepped back. "I saw you slumped in the chair. I wanted to make sure you were okay."

"I fell asleep early morning. You didn't look so hot yourself in your bunk last night." Wilson laughed. "Maybe we're both too old for this all-night excitement. What's going on over at the cabin?"

"One of the officers is with Phil, making breakfast for everyone. I want to take a quick shower and then I'll help with crowd control."

"No, I'd like you to run out to the crime scene now that's it's morning. The officers know what to do when it's time to release the scene, but I'd like you to go out there before that happens. Have a look around for that phone and anything else that looks suspicious. They'll be looking as well but they're not read in on this case the way you are. You said someone is with Phil Beckman?"

"Yes, one of the officers from last night."

"Good. My reports haven't all come back yet except for the fact that our friend Phil has a criminal record. I don't have all the details yet, but he's one of the first people I need to talk to."

"Really? How come we didn't know that about Phil?"

Wilson shrugged. "I don't know. We'll have to find out how well Mr. Daman knows his worker. Unless they know each other very well and are working together."

"What about the officer in the cabin and the others?"

"We have a new shift coming on so everyone can rest, eat, etc. I'm not going to be able to hold everyone much longer than today and I want to start interviewing and getting witness statements as soon as possible so I'll go over to the cabin. Hopefully, they can get more coffee on as soon as possible."

"You got it. I'll be at the scene in a few minutes," Nick said as he turned and left the office. Like the day before, the satellite phone in his pocket vibrated as he walked. He quickly ducked into the woods and answered the phone. "Go."

"There's a large, fallen, hollow tree on your path to the crime scene. I imagine you're headed there sometime today."

"Yes, in a few minutes in fact."

"Something will be waiting for you in the hollow part of the tree. Some of the information you need to figure this out. More later," Luther said before disconnecting the call.

Nick shook his head, looked at the phone. He ran into the cabin to check on Amber. Ten minutes later, he was walking down the path toward the second crime scene. Looking around to make sure no one was watching he found the large, downed tree that Luther had spoken of. Nick reached inside the hollow middle and found a thickly folded white slip of paper. He opened it and scanned the lines quickly. Taking a deep breath, he hurried to the crime scene. He was trying to think of how he could get the information to Wilson without revealing how he had come by it.

Arriving at the crime scene, he saw the yellow tape in the distance. There were several officers and two crime scene investigators moving about the area. One of the investigators was raking a large portion of leaves and ground debris onto a blue tarp that would be brought back to the medical examiner's office.

Nick approached one of the officers. "Everything okay here?"

"And you are?" The officer asked as he stared at Nick.

"Officer Nick Taylor, Misty Point Police Department. I'm working with Detective Wilson on this case and was here last night with him and Dr. Chen when they retrieved the body. Detective Wilson asked me to come back this morning and look at the scene in daylight."

The officer pointed to the area. "The techs are still collecting the debris field. Apparently, they've been asked to collect a wide radius to bring back to the office."

"Do you know if they've found a phone or anything that could be used as a ligature?"

"Not to my knowledge," the officer said as he shook his head. "You can ask the tech but don't touch anything and be careful where you step. Stay out of the defined field."

Nick offered a curt nod. He was aware of crime scene protocol but also aware that this officer was in charge and just doing his job.

Stepping near the tech but staying five feet away, Nick repeated his question to receive a similar answer. There was no sign of the ligature that was used to strangle Dante. Nothing specific except leaves, brush and sticks so far. They would look at everything more closely at the lab and would find animal droppings, insects and the natural things found in the woods, but nothing man made.

Nick offered his thanks and turned. He walked the perimeter for a while as the officer watched, making circles wider and wider until he was twenty feet out. Eventually, he decided to return to camp. On his way back, he paid attention to the path but again did not find anything other than the things that normally belonged in the woods.

Reaching the cabin, Nick went inside to find the officer waiting with several of the executives. Amber was in the common area, looking stressed, but smiled when she saw him.

"The women want to take a shower and have breakfast, but they won't let us leave. They used the small closet toilet for now. Can you help us out?"

Nick walked over to the officer. "Did Wilson come in?"

"Yes, he's over at the mess hall, speaking to someone. He's asked me to wait with the others. I can't escort them to the bathroom and watch the others so we're waiting for more men."

"How about if Amber and I escort the two women to the shower? She can make sure there's no small talk and I'll stand guard outside the door?"

"If you're willing to take the responsibility, sir," the officer said.

"Yes, I will. You can stay here with the others."

"Just three men are left," said the officer. "Mr. Flowers, Mr. Ortiz and Mr. Daman."

"You should be fine with them. I'll help Amber get the women settled." Nick looked up and tilted his head toward the door so Amber would usher the women outside. When they stepped onto the porch, Veronica and Nancy were thankful he had helped to get them out of the cabin.

"It was nasty being stuck in there with those disgusting men," Nancy Rogan said. "Thankfully, we'll be able to go to a real ladies' room."

Veronica burst out laughing. "I can't believe how much appreciation we have for a wooden building with a swinging door, no windows, and ceiling vents covered in wire mesh to keep random animals out. To think I could be home, in Manhattan, in my marbled bathroom with luxury towels and soaps."

"Sorry, but it's the best we can do for today. I'm sure you'll be home soon," Nick said as he frowned at Amber.

He stopped at the outside door of the bathroom, crossed his arms, and said, "I'll be waiting right outside for you ladies. You have fifteen minutes to shower and dress before we go over to the mess hall for breakfast." To Amber he said, "Make sure the conversation stays strictly about weather and kittens."

Veronica rolled her eyes. "If I talk about anything, it'll be about the type of martini I'll be drinking as soon as I get out of this hell hole and back home."

Nancy frowned but followed her into the bathroom.

"Be back in fifteen," Amber said as she gave Nick a little hug. "I'm so thankful you were here for all this."

59

"I've done my time, I'm clean." Wilson sat with Phil Beckman in the back of the kitchen.

"How did you get this job, if you don't mind me asking," Wilson asked sarcastically as he stared at the camp manager.

"You know how it works. When I got out, I went into a prison rehab program and eventually I was able to start a new clean life. That was ten years ago. Check with my parole officer or whomever you want. Clean as a whistle."

"You were in for armed robbery and got out early. How does that happen? I can't check the records because some of them are sealed. What's that all about?"

Phil squirmed in his chair, discomforted by the question. "It's sealed for a reason."

"Humor me. No one is here, no one is listening."

Phil raised his eyebrows and nodded toward the officer in the corner.

Wilson scowled but called out to the officer. "Hey, can you leave us alone for a moment. We're okay here. See if they need any help in the cabin."

The officer gave a curt nod and left the kitchen.

Wilson turned to Phil. "We're all alone now, so talk."

Phil frowned and said, "First of all, you're never alone. The walls have ears, and those ears can get you killed. It just so happens, they saved my life."

"How so?" Wilson asked.

"I was in the joint and I overheard chatter about a possible escape. There was a particular guard they didn't like who rounded at a specific time every night, but no one liked him because he was a Robocop."

"Pardon me?" Wilson asked.

"C'mon, you know, a Robocop. The kind of jail guard that writes up every infraction. Guys hated him."

Wilson nodded. "And?"

"I overheard they were going to try for an escape and kill the Robocop in the process, but the problem was they needed my cell as it had the easiest access to the exit they needed. So, one day, I find out I was going to have the same fate as the Robocop, dead. They wanted me out of the way as fast as possible, plus they could blame the escape on me and say they just took advantage."

"So, what happened?"

"Look, I'm not a proud man and certainly small in stature. I didn't stand a chance, and I'm nobody's patsy, so I sold out. In prison, I was assigned to kitchen duty. That's why I'm so good at camp with all this cooking. Ten people ain't nothing compared to one hundred. Anyway, I got word out that I wanted to see the warden, but they had to make sure it didn't look like I made the request. They did it in a way that made it look like I was in trouble. Robocop and his buddy guards came one night and hustled me out, claimed I tried to poison someone in the kitchen. Sent me to solitary for a week."

Wilson raised his eyebrows. "Go on."

Phil swallowed hard and continued his story. "We spent the week planning. I sang like a bird. Told them all about the plans and made a deal."

"Now I get it. Please continue."

"I'll tell you the rest, but if you ever let this out, I could be a dead man. You can't write this down."

Wilson stared at the man for a moment and nodded. "Nothing you've said is written or taped. If I like your story, it all ends here."

"Good, cause some of these guys will be getting out one day and I don't want to be looking over my shoulder. I did my time and I'm clean."

"Understood," Wilson said.

"The problem was we had to play it as if no one knew. I had to go back to my cell. Robocop kept on his rounds and to make it look real, he gave me a hard time on a regular basis, but if they weren't caught in the act, the information was worth nothing. Anyways, one night, it goes down. Robocop was making his rounds and they manage to get hold of him, get the cell doors open and make their way over to me. All hell breaks loose. I still got shived in the process." Phil lifted his shirt to display a five-inch scar over his left ribs. "Thankfully, they missed my heart and lungs, but the guards were ready and came down on the group. I got sent to the hospital and they got more time in a worse institution. When I healed, I was discharged directly from the hospital with time served. Robocop came in and thanked me personally but nothing's on record to protect me, you know what I mean?"

Wilson nodded but was inclined to believe Phil. He seemed hard working and sincere. "Since you're used to walls with ears and always in the background, have you heard or seen anything we should know about here?"

Phil shook his head. "Nothing specific but if I laid a bet, there's something up with that CEO. He was in here with me yesterday, riding my butt about everything. I'd look at him more closely."

Wilson nodded. "Give me a name to make one confirmatory phone call, then I'll back off."

Phil gave him the name of his parole officer who could connect him with the warden if need be.

Wilson stood up, shook his hand, and said, "I'm looking forward to breakfast."

60

Wilson went to check on everyone's whereabouts and within fifteen minutes, all were gathered in the mess hall. There were many complaints and threats to sue but Wilson wanted to interview everyone again as there was a second crime scene. He needed a little more time to get results from Chen as well as information he had requested about the rest of the guests.

Holding his arms up, he shouted to quiet them down. "Quiet, please." When everyone was looking at him, he explained the situation. "We have another crime scene."

"Oh no," Amber said as she held her hand to her chest.

"We need to get out of here," Veronica whispered. "Or we're dead. There's a good reason people don't go living in the woods. Never again."

Wilson kept talking. "We're waiting until the crime scene is released and for some other information. I'll have to speak with you all again today, but then you'll all be able to use the office phone to call for transportation or your company and prepare to leave if we don't hold you further."

"This is ridiculous," Joe Daman. "My lawyers will be all over you."

"Yes, I'm sure they will," Wilson said. "But I have a feeling they're going to be very busy looking at your company as well."

Daman slammed his fist on the table and looked out the window.

Wilson surveyed the group. He was most curious as to their body language. Phil was in the kitchen preparing the rest of breakfast, but he had already put out the coffee, juice, and tea for the morning.

Bob Flowers looked like he was going to vomit and held his head as if he had a massive headache. Wilson went over to him and noticed he was sweating, and his hands were shaking.

"Are you okay?"

"My head hurts," Bob said as he looked down at the table.

"Are you sick? Do you have a fever?"

Nick walked to the table and sat down across from Bob. "Mind if I ask a question?"

"Yes, I've minded from the minute I got here. What the hell do you want now?"

Nick leaned forward so only he and Wilson could hear. "When was the last time you had a drink?"

Bob looked up. "Seriously?"

"Yes, seriously. Did you run out of whiskey?"

Bob's face lightened for a moment. "Do you have any? You must have a stash here somewhere."

"Do you normally drink before breakfast?"

Bob looked up at him. His eyes were bloodshot, his hair stood on end. "Only when I need a pick me up. Do you have anything or not? I'll take anything."

Nick nodded. "I may have something. I'm going to talk to Detective Wilson and get back to you."

"Please make it fast." Bob said as he held his head to stop the pounding.

Nick pulled Wilson over to the side of the room. "I've been watching this guy since he arrived. Between his flask and the bottle of Jack in his bunk I think he's finished everything he had and is starting withdrawal. He may need some medical attention soon but before he goes, I want to let you know about something I found out."

"Oh? Like what?"

Nick was unsure how to let Wilson know about the information he had. He wanted to tell him he had researched the executives before he arrived but then Wilson would ask him why he had been holding out all this time. He would never reveal Megan or Luther were aware of the situation or had contributed. Besides being seriously questioned by Wilson, he'd lose his job at the Misty Point Police Department as well.

"I don't know how significant this is, but I found out that Bob Flowers used to work at another company with Joe Daman. They haven't talked to each other much since they arrived, but they did work together years ago. I thought you might want to explore that before Flowers gets carted off to the hospital."

"And you know this how?"

Nick stared at him. "Please don't ask me how I know, just verify and confirm."

Wilson stared back for a few seconds. "I don't like it, but I'm not going to question you. Let's talk to Flowers first and then Daman. He can stew for a bit yet."

Nick nodded. "Let's get Bob to the back of the kitchen for privacy. Maybe Phil has a little cooking wine he can have before we call an ambulance."

The men walked over to Bob Flowers. Nick leaned down. "Hey, Bob. Why don't you come with us into the kitchen. We'll get you something to eat right away. It's possible Phil has wine or a beer in there. We'll ask."

Bob looked up with suspicion in his bloodshot eyes. "If it gets me a drink, I'll go." Together the small group went inside the kitchen as Wilson nodded to another officer to keep an eye on the group in the dining room. They sat Bob down at a small table used for peeling vegetables. Nick asked Phil for a cup of coffee for Bob.

Wilson sat in front of him. "Bob, we want to get you help so you can feel better. I'm going to call someone soon, but I need to ask you one thing. You know that when we have a crime scene, we have to check everyone out, right?"

"Whatever, I haven't done anything except drink," Bob said. "I played horseshoes with Albert yesterday afternoon right here in camp."

"Do you remember what the score was?"

"No friggin idea," Bob said as he shook his head. "What's the problem?"

"Nothing really. I wanted to ask you a question about Mr. Daman."

"Who?"

"He's the CEO who is in charge of this retreat," Nick said. "He's been talking to Amber in the cabin."

Recognition dawned on Bob's face. "Oh, that guy. Why ask me? Why don't you ask her?"

Wilson looked at Nick with a frown. "We checked on everyone's history and the records came back that he was your boss at one point. You both worked for a different company back then."

Bob shook his head, then stopped. "You know, now that you mention it, the guy did look kind of familiar. I was wondering about that, but then who cares, right?"

"So, you don't remember working in his company or talking to him before this retreat."

Bob shook his head. "No way, some of these companies are large. You never meet the leadership. They have no idea who you are." Bob laughed. "Unless it's one of the companies that fired me for being drunk on the job but they usually don't put that on your record so you can't sue them."

Nick nodded. "Got it." He tapped Wilson on the arm and beckoned him over to a bank of tall steel refrigerators. "I don't think we have anything to hold him here. Either he truly doesn't remember Daman or he's a hell of an actor if they came here with an agenda to get rid of Felix."

Wilson shook his head. "I agree. I think the only thing he's concentrating on is alcohol. We'll have to pull Daman in next. Even if he admits he knows Flowers, I have nothing to tie either one to the murder. The guy could be involved in corporate espionage for all I know but I can't prove a thing. I'm going to have to let these people leave soon, but before I do, I have to talk to Chen. I want to know if he found anything definitive and see if he can released the crime scene. I also want to check with my office to see what our investigation found. If there's anything else you want to tell me, make sure you do it soon."

"I'll let you know, but my sources are reliable."

"Okay, escort Bob back to the dining room. Get him some breakfast," Wilson said. "I want to talk to Daman first, then I'll call for the rest."

"You got it," Nick said as he watched Phil hand Bob a big plate of food.

egan walked across the beach as she watched the dogs play on the sand. They loved to run back and forth toward the waves as they crashed. Another favorite pastime was chasing the seagulls off the sand. It was a lovely October day. Warm enough to relax and enjoy the setting but quiet and restful now that the summer guests had all gone home.

Breakfast with Marie was delicious. Marie didn't pry as to the subject of all her research and was satisfied that it was to help Nick. Although Megan had initially fought the idea of a nap, she followed Marie's advice. She went upstairs and took a hot shower. Realizing her worries were not going to change the situation she tried to relax. Waking three hours later, she was amazed at how fast and deeply she had slept. Her dreams had been full of images of Nick as well as Jonathan.

She worried about Nick but trusted in Luther's opinion that she would hear from him today. She didn't expect to hear back from Jonathan for a while and she sincerely hoped that Teddy was okay. Either way, when the dust settled, she would do what she had to do to have a greater awareness of all aspects of the foundation.

As she watched the waves, she was eager to get back to the house to see if the final information she requested had arrived. Hopefully, it would reveal something useful. Luther would check in soon so her results would get to Nick, and he could wrap things up and come back to Misty Manor. Halloween was only a few weeks away and Megan was hoping she and Nick could decorate Misty Manor for the holiday and fall season. Perhaps another visit to the attic would be in order to find previous decorations.

Megan called to the dogs and headed toward the porch. As she began to climb the steps, she spied Smokey rubbing against one of the rockers that sat on the porch. She unlocked the front door and went into the library to check her computer.

Thankfully it was a Tuesday, and the office she had requested the information from was open. She opened her browser, checked her email, and was rewarded with several pages of data. She wasn't sure how relevant it was to what was happening at the camp, but she printed the four pages and read through them. Summarizing the information, she typed a page of specific notes and placed it in an envelope.

Megan wished there was an easier way she could contact Luther. She had a cell number he had given her during a past emergency and she used it now. Realizing he kept information as generic as possible, she made her text simple.

Final package received. Please pick up and deliver.

SHE DIDN'T RECEIVE a response but knew someone would be there shortly and within fifteen minutes, Luther appeared at her window once again. Instead of opening the window and risking Marie feeling the breeze, she took the envelope and slid out the front door to the wraparound porch. She continued walking until she was at the side of the house without a window for privacy. Luther anticipated her response and met her there. For some reason she shivered as she met him. The breeze was beginning to kick up and although the day was cooling off, she knew it had nothing to do with her chill.

"I hope this information helps Nick," she said as she handed over the envelope. "It's not sealed if you want to read through."

"Thank you," Luther said. "I'll get this to him right away. I'm sure it will help. Keep cool, he'll be home with you soon."

"Thank you, Luther." She tentatively reached out and gave him a quick squeeze although she knew he was not someone who routinely hugged other people. "Take good care of him."

"No worries," he said as he turned and hopped off the porch.

Megan sighed, wrapped her arms around herself and went back into Misty Manor.

62

Nick watched as everyone in the mess hall sat at various tables eating their breakfast. The executives looked tired and distressed. Nick couldn't blame them. None of the executives had been happy to come to the retreat to begin with. Amber had been anxious but determined to do her best. No one could have predicted what would happen and no one had a solid explanation up to this point either.

Amber came to his side. "Nick, what's going on exactly? We're not being told anything."

Nick looked at Amber and smiled. Like the others, she was tired and had circles under her eyes. The little sleep anyone was able to get was not restorative.

"We're looking to see if anyone has a criminal record or any past relationships with each other. Wilson wants to speak with them first. Everyone will have to be reinterviewed but with the increased knowledge, we may be able to flush something out. Once everyone is questioned and signed a witness statement, they'll be able to make arrangements to leave."

"Does Daman know that?"

Nick looked over at the agitated CEO and then back at Amber. "I think he's figuring it out now but basically, the conference is over. What effect that has on his company or reputation is something he'll have to deal with."

"Yikes, I hope he doesn't blame me," Amber said with a shudder.

"What happened here has nothing to do with you. We don't know the identity of the killer or the true motive at this point, but I doubt you could have done anything that would have changed anything either way. As I recall you were hired as an ambassador to walk them through their schedule of activities, lectures, dining, and recreation. We weren't asked to be here as babysitters, and we had no hand in accepting the guests or making the arrangements. As far as I'm concerned, it's all on him and Portal Health."

Amber made a face and had her arms crossed in front of her. "Just remind me of that when this is all over and he wants to talk about my role."

"Let me know when and where and I'll be happy to attend the meeting with you."

The satellite phone in Nick's pocket started to vibrate. "Excuse me." He walked to the wall, pulled it out of his pocket and read the message.

New information in tree hollow. Pick up asap.

NICK WHIRLED around when he heard the door of the mess hall open. Wilson walked in and motioned for Nick to join him in the kitchen. Together they walked into the back room and found Phil at the stove.

"What's up?" Phil asked concerned with the expression on Wilson's face.

"I got hold of your parole officer."

"And?" The broken egg he was holding began to drip onto the griddle.

"I was able to confirm enough of your story to let you leave the camp at this point. Your parole officer evidently thinks very highly of you."

Phil let out a deep breath. "Great. I didn't have any doubts, but you never know these days, right?'

"True, so you can pack up and go whenever you're ready and you have a ride. I can have an officer escort you to the office to call someone to pick you up."

Phil smiled and nodded. "Thanks, but I think I'm going to stay here for the day. I'll finish breakfast and get the place cleaned up. I'll start lunch for anyone that's here." Phil looked back at the griddle. "It's not like I have a specific place to be, and I've found I like the camp. It's relaxing. I think I'll try to spend more time camping in the state park after the winter."

Wilson nodded. "Okay, thanks for helping out."

Wilson and Nick returned to the dining room but huddled in the corner as Wilson made himself a cup of coffee. "I've got to get witness statements for the time of the second crime from each of these executives. The retreat is over. It's time to clear the area and do the rest of the detective work on the outside."

"Did Chen do the post?"

Wilson nodded as he gulped his coffee. "He confirmed the guy was strangled. He found plant material in the wound and a strong vine in the debris field with some blood on it, so it looks like our killer used the vine as a ligature."

Nick raised his eyebrows as he listened. "Wow, can he get anything off of that?"

"He's going to try to recover anything that would help link us to the killer. He's checking for DNA with the blood. There were some cuts on Dante's neck that were probably opened by the ligature, so the blood could be Dante's, or it could be from a cut on the killer's hand for instance."

"Maybe, we should be checking everyone's hands," Nick mused. "Anything else? Time of death?"

"He lists the time of death somewhere in the afternoon which is another reason I know that Beckman couldn't have done it. I know he was here cooking and getting dinner ready. If you recall, they had been sequestered in the cabin after a meal and Chen said Dante's stomach contents and timing were consistent with what was served at that last meal. Immediate testing didn't reveal any alcohol or drugs. Chen will wait on the full tox screen for anything else."

"What about the crime scene?" Nick asked as he watched the detective fill another cup of coffee.

"He doesn't think they'll find anything more that would help. He sent some of the crime scene techs back with rakes to see if they can find the phone somewhere in the area. I had our IT department try to ping the phone, but no luck so far. We have other detectives reaching out to Dante's family for the notification, and to ask if any family or friends received any texts or calls from him around that time.

"We can go to the phone company to check, but that would take some time and it would be difficult to recall photos from the server. The best chance would have been recovering the phone from the crime scene."

"Can I go and check the scene a final time?"

Wilson stared at Nick for a moment and shrugged. "Suit yourself. You'd just be sitting around here watching me talk to these people and getting them to sign a statement."

"Great, I'll head out now," Nick said as he nodded to the detective.

"Nick," Wilson called after him.

Nick stopped and turned around. "Yes?"

"When you get back, make sure you share any other bits of information you have before I let anyone leave. Got me?"

Nick nodded with a grin and left the mess hall.

63

Nick hurried down the path toward the crime scene. On the way, he ducked into the woods to retrieve the information from the tree hollow. Looking around to make sure no one was watching, he reached in and pulled out the folded piece of paper. He quickly scanned the info and raised an eyebrow.

Turning, he stepped back onto the wooded path and went to the crime scene. The yellow tape was still wrapped around the trees, but he could see the entire area had been raked clean to the dirt and tree roots. The techs had also raked twenty feet out on all sides.

There was no mention that a cell phone had been found so either the killer took it, or it was trashed elsewhere in the forest. Repeated attempts to ping the phone hadn't helped with location, so it was either destroyed or uncharged.

To appease himself, Nick did a structured search of the ground in and outside of the crime scene to see if anything was missed, but he found nothing and returned to camp.

Opening the door to the mess hall, he found the executives glumly sitting at the tables or leaning on the wall. Phil walked out with a large, fresh urn of coffee. He made sure to resupply the sugar and creamers, as well as snacks that sat on the side table.

Nick walked into the back of the kitchen and saw Detective Wilson sitting at a table with Joe Daman. They were engaged in conversation and Daman was angrily pointing at Wilson.

"I'd suggest you get your finger out of my face immediately or we'll have this conversation somewhere more official," Wilson said while holding Daman with an icy glare.

"This whole retreat and investigation were botched. I'll have your badge."

Wilson sat back in his chair and scowled. "If I don't have you arrested and charged first for assault. Now I suggest you answer my questions."

Daman's face was red with rage, and he pounded the table. He turned his face to the wall before turning back to Wilson. "What do you want now? I've told you everything I know."

"It's come to our attention that you and Bob Flowers have worked together in the past."

"Who?"

"Bob Flowers, the gentleman who was just in here?"

"The alcoholic?"

"I'm not a doctor so I can't make a judgement, but our investigation shows he was under your employ in the past. Do you deny that?"

"How the hell do I know? Do you think I meet every peon that works for the company? As far as I'm concerned, I've never seen the guy before this week. What does that have to do with anything?"

"We're just wondering if there's any other executives you've worked with or past grudges we should know about?"

"That's the most ridiculous thing I've ever heard. I don't have a relationship with any of these people except Amber Montgomery, who is currently an employee, although I may be making a change there soon."

Nick took a deep breath and crossed his arms in front of him. Joe Daman looked up at him and noticed the tall, broad-shouldered officer with bulging biceps and fierce scowl. He stopped talking.

"One last question," Wilson asked. "Can you tell me where you were yesterday afternoon?"

"Either I was working with my attorney, or I was here."

"You don't remember which it was or when?"

"Do I look like the sort of man who needs to punch a clock, Detective?"

Nick turned and walked a few feet into the room before he turned around and went back.

Wilson watched him as he looked back at Daman and said, "I've had this park closed to the public. How have you been getting in and out?"

"I'm in great shape. I'm a runner. I parked my car on the shoulder of the main road, and I hiked in and out each time."

Wilson smiled. "I'll need your attorney's name and number to corroborate your story. Once your statement is typed and signed, you can call your attorney to pick you up unless you have another arrangement. Until then, please wait in the mess hall."

Daman shoved his chair backwards. He pulled his wallet from his pants, looked through for one of his attorney's cards and flipped it onto the table in front of Wilson. He then turned and stalked out of the kitchen.

Wilson looked up at Nick and shook his head. "I was hoping he'd say something incriminating so I could arrest him."

64

Megan tried to keep busy as the afternoon wore on. She hoped that Luther was able to get the information to Nick and this whole nightmare would end soon. She wouldn't feel comfortable until he was back at Misty Manor. She decided right there and then, she would ask him to work for the foundation. They would be able to use a security detail in many situations. The foundation could offer him a good salary. He would fight it, but at least she would know he'd be safe.

When her cell phone started ringing, she jumped up and grabbed it off the desk. "Hello?" Megan hadn't taken the time to check the caller ID and was disappointed the caller was not Nick.

"Megan, how are you?"

"Teddy! How are you? Where have you been? I've been trying to reach you for days."

"I know, my dear, and I must apologize for my absence. I'll tell you directly, that I have been in the hospital for some tests."

"Teddy, are you alright?"

"I'm fine. It was only supposed to be a day, but the first test had some findings that the medical team wanted to check further, so I was asked to stay." Teddy laughed. "I was told I had to have the workup immediately. Everything is fine. Just medication for now so you needn't worry any further."

"I'm happy to hear that," Megan said. "I'd like to discuss the foundation with you, but I don't think now is the time. Perhaps we can make an appointment when you've been home a bit?'

"That sounds grand," Teddy said. "I did have a brief conversation with Jonathan. He told me about the homeless shelter and Pastor Lee. I agree it sounds like a very worthwhile cause and if it will help with collaboration between the hospital and town police, I believe the community will benefit. It will be top of the agenda for our next board meeting and I'm sure the committee will approve all suggestions. Besides that, your grandmother approved of the shelter several years ago and would haunt me if we didn't continue."

"That sounds great," Megan said. "Perhaps we can have a celebration at the center to help spread the word in the community when everything is settled."

"That sounds like a grand idea. The board meeting is next week so any time after that will be fine, I'm sure."

"I'll be happy when we can call Pastor Lee and plan everything. In the meantime, I'll look forward to the board meeting." Megan paused for a few seconds. "Did you speak with Jonathan about his plans?"

"Yes, we spoke a little. We have more planning to do. He needs to unpack and get settled. Once he relaxes, we'll be able to discuss the future."

"Good, I'm glad. I want him to be happy." There was an awkward pause before Megan spoke again. "I'm going to go, Teddy. I'm waiting to hear from Nick. There's been some terrible drama happening in the state park and I need to make sure he's okay."

"Absolutely, my dear. I'll be in touch before next week's board meeting so you can approve the agenda before we meet."

"Thank you, Teddy. Please take care of yourself. I need you."

Teddy was quiet for a moment. "Of course. Thank you, Megan. Goodbye."

65

"We'd better get out there," Wilson said to Nick as he pushed his chair in. "All these witness interviews and we have nothing."

"Wait, I have another piece of information."

"And you don't want me to ask how you know?" Wilson stared at Nick without smiling.

"No, I'm sorry I can't tell you that. I don't know if it's going to make a difference in the case, but I want you to know what I found out in case it does. I think it's important."

"Okay, let's have it then," Wilson said as he waited to hear what Nick had to say.

Nick spent the next five minutes telling Wilson about what he learned. He didn't pull out the paper because he didn't want to admit he had a satellite phone or that Luther and Megan were offering information.

Wilson nodded as he listened. "That's interesting because our investigation didn't show that information."

"All charges were dropped," Nick said. "Maybe everything was buried."

"Well, either you've got a database we don't normally use or what you just told me is unsubstantiated. I guess we'll find out one way or another. Let's go."

The two officers walked out into the main dining area. Scanning the tables, they saw the remaining executives sitting at tables.

Bob Flowers was sitting with his head down on a back table. Alberto Ortiz was sitting at a table playing solitaire with a deck of cards. Veronica was standing by a large window staring out into the woods. Nancy Rogan sat with her arms folded and a sour look on her face. Joe Daman sat backwards on a wooden chair, holding his head with his right arm. Amber stood anxiously in a corner watching Phil drying dishes at the counter. An officer stood near the door with his arms folded. Nick and Wilson walked into the middle of the room.

Wilson got everyone's attention. "Thank you all for being so cooperative. I only have a couple more interviews and witness statements to complete and you'll all be released for now. We may have need to ask more questions in the future, but the conference is almost over.

"My prayers have been answered," Veronica said as she turned from the window. "Can I go next so I can go to the cabin and pack? Pretty please?"

Wilson smiled despite himself. "Yes, I'll take you next."

They turned when they heard a gagging noise and witnessed Bob Flowers vomiting in the corner of the room.

"Oh no," Amber said, her eyes widened. Phil came from around the corner. He placed a glass pitcher on the table and ran toward Bob with a towel and cold water.

Bob looked up as he wiped the front of his shirt. "Permission to go to the bathroom, please."

Wilson looked at the officer and nodded to get Bob out of the room. The officer helped Bob up and helped him walk toward the exit. As they passed, Wilson said, "Go to the office on the way back and call an ambulance to take him to Coastal Community Hospital." The officer nodded and kept walking.

Alberto bit his lip as he watched the pair leave. He turned to Veronica and said, "I've never seen him this bad at work."

Veronica rolled her eyes. "That's because he does most of his drinking in his office."

Joe Daman shook his head. "I can't believe I'm stuck here with these trashy people."

"Excuse me?" Veronica said as her eyes shot daggers at him.

"Is that all you people do? No wonder you were sent here. Alcohol, cursing, drugs, sex, except for goody two-shoes over here," Daman said as he pointed toward Alberto.

"Who are you to judge?" Veronica asked.

Nancy Rogan started laughing. "It's true, you did have sex with him in the woods, but then again Dante would have sex with anything that moved."

"How would you know we had sex in the woods? Were you spying on us?" Veronica spun around and turned her fierce stare at Nick. "Or did you go blabbing that you found us in a compromised position."

Nick raised his hands. "I didn't tell anyone anything about Sunday night. Don't blame me."

Veronica turned back to Nancy and began to mock her. "Dante has sex with everyone. He probably would have had sex with you too, if you weren't such a bitch all the time."

"It's one thing to have sex with someone you've just met. It's another to take photos," Nancy said.

"It's none of your business what we did, Missy," Veronica said as she placed her hands on her hips and stood in front on Nancy.

Nick whispered to Wilson. "How did Nancy know they took photos, unless...?" Their attention was called back to the altercation between Nancy and Veronica.

Nancy was yelling at Veronica, "How dare you call me a bitch."

"Oh c'mon, you started yelling the minute you got here. I saw you arguing with Felix Cooper after lunch on Sunday just before you practically dragged him with you into the woods." Veronica suddenly stopped yelling and as she realized what she had witnessed, her hands flew to her mouth. "You killed him. You killed them both. You took the phone."

Nick and Wilson both moved immediately to get to Nancy, but

before they did, Nancy jumped up and grabbed Veronica by the hair. She held her in front of her like a shield. Nancy then grabbed a knife from her pocket that she had used at lunch and dug the tip into Veronica's neck.

"Don't move. If anyone moves a muscle, I'll jam this knife so far into her carotid you'll see blood spurting for days."

Veronica screamed. Nick and Wilson stopped. "Just hold on. Let's discuss this. Do not hurt that woman," Wilson yelled.

"You're right," Nancy said with a deep laugh. "I'll need a hostage for at least five minutes to get the hell out of here." Nancy yanked Veronica's hair and head back further and started inching toward the door. Wilson and Nick stood their ground until she was near enough to jump but out of nowhere, Alberto body slammed both Nancy and Veronica. They all fell backward toward the ground pulling one of the tables over with them.

Wilson and Nick jumped forward to tackle Nancy, but she pushed Veronica off her, grabbed the glass pitcher and brought it down over Wilson's head as he lunged. Wilson staggered to the ground as Nancy got up and ran for the door, pushing Amber into Nick so they both hit the wall as she went by. Joe Daman cowered on the other side of the room.

Nick turned to Amber. "Are you all right?"

She had a hand on her head. "Yes, I'm fine."

As Alberto comforted Veronica in the corner, Nick got up and raced out the door after Nancy Rogan.

66

N ancy took off down the path away from the cabin and toward the parking lot. She saw multiple police cars parked at different angles near the office and veered away from where the officer was waiting with an ambulance for Bob. Taking a right turn, she tore down the trail toward the ocean.

Nick could see her in the distance and ran as fast as he could to chase her through the wood. His lungs burned and his right leg was numb, but he kept going so he wouldn't lose sight of her. He prayed he would catch her and feared that he was losing ground.

There was a small stream that crossed the trail. Nancy tried to jump over the stream, but her foot landed on a patch of wet leaves on the opposite bank which caused her to fall. By the time she scrambled to her feet and started running again, Nick had gained serious ground. He was able to jump the stream without difficulty and continue to chase Nancy. He realized how seriously he was out of shape, but he was able to keep up with her.

Nearing the opening to the beach, Nick rounded a bend in the path and tripped over a tree branch that was across the trail. He landed on the carpeted path face first. As he rolled over, he saw

Nancy standing over him holding another large branch. She aimed for his head and brought the limb toward his face, but Nick was able to roll out of the way before it slammed onto the path. She dropped her weapon and took off down the trail to continue her run toward the ocean.

Nick scrambled to his feet and took off again as he chased her. They were fifty feet from the opening to the beach and Nick could now hear other officers behind him as they ran to catch up to the chase.

Nancy reached the opening in the trees that led to the sand. She went through and began to run across the beach. Each step threw a spray of sand back toward Nick. Averting his eyes, Nick ran across the beach, continuing to close the gap. His training and numerous hours on beach patrol had prepared him for this exact sort of run.

Nearing the ocean's edge, Nancy ran toward a jetty that separated the beach from a boat access ramp. Once she crossed the jetty, she would be able to run up the ramp and out onto the main highway which would make the chase that much harder.

Six feet from the jetty, Nick lunged forward, thankful for his football days in college and tackled Nancy around the knees. She fell forward onto the sand and immediately began kicking Nick's face with her feet. She broke free for just a moment and began crawling toward the jetty, ready to cross and distance herself. Nick was just getting up as two officers ran past him and pushed her back to the ground. Within seconds they had her hands cuffed behind her and were picking her up. One of the officers had radioed ahead and a patrol car pulled up on the boat ramp where Nancy Rogan was loaded into the back seat and driven to the police station.

Nick took a few minutes to catch his breath as he watched the police car drive off and then turned to walk back to camp. As he crossed the beach he looked up and saw the lighthouse in the distance and couldn't wait to get back to Misty Manor and be with Megan. He had wanted to be away from there, and now after three days, couldn't wait to get back. Nick entered the wood and retraced the trail to return to camp. When he entered the mess hall, he spotted Wilson with an ice pack on his head. Another officer was standing at the door. Amber and Joe Daman were in one corner of the room. Veronica and Alberto sat at a table with Phil Beckman.

Nick looked at Wilson and said, "We got her. This retreat is officially over."

67

Two weeks later, there was a celebration and small ceremony at the homeless shelter to officially mark the grant bestowed by the Stanford Foundation. Marie cooked a large variety of hors d'oeuvres for the occasion. Drinks and a beautiful cake had been ordered. Megan stood with her hand wrapped around Nick's arm. Beside them stood Georgie, Doogie, Amber, and Tommy.

Pastor Lee was shaking the hand of Jonathan Brandon Carter. Teddy was standing beside them and looked in good health. Mayor Davenport was standing behind them scowling.

The celebration was winding down and the board members who had attended the celebration were beginning to leave, as well as the photographer from the local newspaper.

Looking up, Nick suddenly waved when he saw Detective Wilson enter the shelter. Nick welcomed him to the group and made introductions all around.

"How are you feeling? How's the head?" Nick asked with a smile.

Wilson rubbed the top of his head as he laughed. "My wife is hopeful I had some sense knocked into me and will change my ways. I'm not optimistic." Wilson looked around and noting there were no more guests, turned to Nick and Amber. "I wanted to thank you for all your help and let you know that everything is settled."

"Thank goodness," Amber said. "I don't think it's privileged information anymore as the papers have carried a lot of information, but would you care to fill us in on the motives?"

Wilson looked at Nick and nodded. "It was Nick who gave us the final clue although he won't disclose how he got the information."

Megan felt Nick squeeze her hand.

"It seems that Nancy Rogan and Felix Cooper had a history of working together in another hospital. They both worked for IT and were responsible for gathering information on patients, physicians, insurance companies, as well as other data. They both admitted their specific job was data mining and therefore they were responsible for a lot of information. That type of job and employees always need to be held accountable. Felix held that the reason was strictly for data analytics which is common in healthcare and other industries. For example, they can track how many opioid prescriptions a particular doctor writes and which surgeon has more complications. The data would also inform the user about the most common diagnosis in the patient population as well as the most used insurance, most common type of cancer, and whether there is a cancer cluster in a particular geographic area. It may reveal most common tests used in the emergency room. The application and uses are quite endless really."

"What happened between Nancy and Felix?" Amber asked.

"As Nick found out, there is a very fine line between mining data for analytics and for criminal purposes. At some point, Felix Cooper began to suspect that Nancy Rogan was selling her data and he put in a whistleblower claim. Unfortunately, there was not enough proof to make a criminal case, but they were both let go and she had a large smear on her reputation."

"What would she be selling?" Amber asked as she turned to Wilson.

"Oh, everything from simple identity theft which is most common when patients die. That's one of the biggest areas of identity theft. Your birthday, social security number and driver's license are all someone needs. Then you can sell credit card information, insurance information, medical information, passwords, and direct bank account numbers just to name a few. Identity theft and fraudulent information are big business now. Everything is digital so data mining is a large area of cybertheft. Whoever has that type of access must realize the responsibility. They could also involve partners and hold records for ransom.

"At any rate, Felix was reemployed at a medical supply company and Nancy Rogan was working for a medical record company. I'm sure they recognized each other right away. Nancy might have killed Felix in revenge, or she may have been on to a new scheme. She hasn't told us what specifically instigated Felix's murder yet, but she has admitted the murders."

"And Dante?" Amber continued while looking at Wilson.

"We suspect Dante was killed for his photos of the first day and probably caught a snap of Nancy and Felix arguing in the woods. It didn't matter in the end though once Veronica remembered them walking off and Nancy admitted as much."

"That's all very frightening," Amber said with a shudder. "You think you're meeting six educated executives and look what happens."

Wilson looked at Amber and Nick as he asked. "What was the follow up on your end?"

Nick sighed. "From what I've heard, lives have changed. We know Nancy Rogan is in jail and will be tried for murder. Bob Flowers was admitted to the hospital and has now gone into rehab for his alcoholism. Felix Cooper and Dante Valentino both had funerals and Megan, Amber, and I attended those."

Wilson then added. "We did a follow up at Antacus Pharmaceuticals and from what I understand, Veronica Lane was promoted to VP and is happily dating the CEO, Dominic King. Alberto Ortiz was also promoted, made employee of the year, and is now VP of the HR Division in charge of stress management, workplace fatigue, compassion, and trauma. I believe Alberto managed to hire Phil Beckman full time to help him with day seminars for the company employees."

"That's great," Amber said. "He was a nice man."

Wilson turned to Amber. "Speaking of trauma, how are you doing?"

Amber nodded but was a bit teary as she spoke. "I was trying to do a good job but who knew this would happen. I had a loud discussion with Joe Daman and quit my job, but the company asked me to take a leave of absence and think about things. I have six months to decide what I want to do and for them to see if the company is still standing. I guess they're worried about lawsuits and such. They're waiting for the fallout now."

"What about our buddy, Joe Daman?" Nick asked with a scowl.

"I don't think he did anything illegal," Amber said. "He's just a jerk. At any rate, he's in charge and will need to deal with whatever Portal Health is held responsible for. The lawsuits have already started coming in. The key stakeholders are out for his blood and his reputation has been tarnished forever. No golden parachute for him this time."

"Couldn't happen to a nicer guy," Nick said as he shook his head.

Wilson looked at his watch. "I'd better be off. My wife is expecting me home. It was great meeting everyone."

Nick leaned forward and shook Wilson's hand. "I'm hoping to see you again sometime soon, but not in an official capacity."

Wilson nodded. "I agree. I heard you're back with the Misty Point Police Department full time. Congratulations."

"Yes, after that week, I passed my treadmill test and the doctor agreed to let me go back full time. Captain Davis is not as happy. He'll want me on desk duty forever." Nick laughed. "Maybe we can all meet up for dinner one day."

"That would be lovely," Megan agreed.

As Wilson left, Pastor Lee, Teddy, Jonathan, and Marie made their way over. "Marie did a great job," Pastor Lee said as he beamed at her. "Once again, I'd like to thank all of you and the Stanford Foundation for making this happen."

"Our pleasure," Megan said. "The supplies and linens have all arrived. The dry pantry is stocked, and Marie is ready to cook. You just let us know what you need."

"The police department is eager to help the shelter and the community."

Pastor Lee smiled. "All positive vibes."

The group laughed, congratulated each other on the success of the day, said their goodbyes and went their separate ways.

Jonathan pulled Megan to the side. "Thank you for helping me get situated here. I was lost with Dad not being around and the move to another country."

"I understand," Megan said with a smile.

"You and Nick look very happy."

"We are. We're not settled yet but we're working our future out," Megan said as she looked over at Nick speaking with Pastor Lee. She turned back to Jonathan. "What did you decide to do?"

"I'll be working with my dad for a while. I need to learn his accounts and get some experience inside the American court system."

"What about the car?"

Jonathan grinned ear to ear and finally spoke. "I bought myself a baby blue convertible Porsche. I couldn't resist."

Megan shook her head and laughed. "And Teddy is, okay?"

Jonathan nodded. "For now. If he takes his medicine and follows his doctor's advice, he should be fine. I'll let you know if he misbehaves, and we can both go after him."

"Thank you. He's more than just an estate attorney to the family and so are you."

"Thank you, Megan," Jonathan said as he gave her a quick peck on the cheek and left the shelter.

Nick had his arm around Megan as he walked her out to the car. He pulled the passenger door open on his Camaro and helped her into her seat before he walked around the front and got situated at the wheel.

"It's a shame Luther couldn't be here today," Megan said as she watched Nick put his sunglasses on.

"From what I hear, he's got a private assignment, so I don't think he's in town right now. But you know Luther, never one for a crowd. The man likes to be invisible."

"That's for sure. Someday, you'll have to share how you two met."

Nick laughed. "I don't know if I can do that. Besides, I'm more concerned with my history with you." He leaned over and kissed Megan. "I thought I'd never make it back. I can't wait to go back to Misty Manor. I was only gone for three days but it seemed a lifetime."

"For me as well, Nick. You're sure you won't consider my offer to work for the Stanford Foundation?"

Nick smiled as he looked at Megan. "Not yet. You and Amber can discuss that for now, but I love you all the more for trying to protect me."

"Very well, then."

He kissed her again, more slowly this time. "It's a gorgeous day for October. Let's go hit the beach."

Megan smiled and hugged Nick around the shoulders. "I thought you would never ask."

ABOUT THE AUTHOR

Linda Rawlins is an American writer of mystery fiction best known for her Misty Point Mystery Series, including Misty Manor, Misty Point, Misty Winter, Misty Treasure and Misty Revenge. She is also known for her Rocky Meadow Mystery Series, including The Bench, Fatal Breach, Sacred Gold as week as an independent novel, Midnight Shift.

Linda loved to read as a child and started writing her first mystery novel in fifth grade. She then went on to study science, medicine, and literature, eventually graduating from medical school and establishing her career in medicine.

Linda Rawlins lives in New Jersey with her husband, her family and spoiled dog. She loves spending time at the beach as well as visiting the mountains of Vermont. She is an active member of Mystery Writers of America. As a member of Sisters in Crime, Linda was the President of the Central Jersey Chapter for 2022, 2020, 2019 and the VP in 2018.

amazon.com/Linda-Rawlins/e/B00C4TPXF2
facebook.com/lindarawlinsauthor
instagram.com/lindarawlinsauthor
twitter.com/lrl8
tiktok.com/@lindarawlinsauthor

Made in the USA
Las Vegas, NV
20 October 2022

57798407R00142